USA TODAY BESTSELLING AUTHOR

NANCY WARREN

A ROLLING SCONE

THE GREAT WITCHES BAKING SHOW
BOOK 3

ISBN: ebook 978-1-928145-72-1

ISBN: print 978-1-928145-73-8

Cover Design by Lou Harper of Cover Affairs

INTRODUCTION

Butter, sugar, flour — and Death!

British amateur bakers must turn out the perfect scone in this week's filming of The Great British Baking Contest.

But fledgling witch Poppy is losing her concentration as she gets closer to discovering more of her own history at Broomewode Hall, a postcard pretty manor house in Somerset, England. However, someone is warning her to leave as she's in danger.

Can she keep her cool while solving mysteries, working on her witch skills, and still turn out a decent scone?

Taste this culinary cozy mystery series from USA Today Bestselling author Nancy Warren. Each book is a standalone mystery, though the books are linked. They offer good, clean fun, and, naturally, recipes.

~

The best way to keep up with new releases and special offers is to join Nancy's newsletter at **nancywarren.net or** www.-facebook.com/groups/NancyWarrenKnitwits

A ROLLING SCONE

CHAPTER 1

It was hard to get too excited about baking the perfect scone when I'd been warned I was in terrible danger. All week long I'd been having nightmares. The cryptic note I'd received at the end of last week's filming of The Great British Baking Contest played across my mind in a repeating flashing sequence.

Dearest Poppy,

You are in terrible danger. You shouldn't be here. I'm begging you: Do something to get yourself voted off of the show next week. Otherwise I fear it will be too late. Please heed my words.

Had I considered taking the anonymous letter writer's advice? Maybe for a few minutes, but then I got mad. Who sent a person a note like that with no supporting evidence? No hints on what specifically to watch out for? And, oh, yeah, no signature. I'd read, and re-read and studied the message in between practicing baking and working at my real graphic design job.

The first puzzling thing was the tone. If someone wanted

me off of the show, then why address me as "Dearest Poppy"? Dearest made it seem like they were my friend or cared about me deeply in some way. I only ever wrote "dearest" when I was writing emails to my mom and dad, or maybe in a text to my best friend, Gina. And then there was the element of real fear behind those words: *terrible danger...I'm begging you...too late.* It felt like a genuine warning. But why not tell me what the danger *was*? Or when it might be coming?

I'd ruled out it being from my ghost pal Gerry's bored and warped mind; he still couldn't work out how to grip a pen. But I couldn't stop myself from wondering if it had been from one of the other bakers on the show. Did anyone want to win *The Great British Baking Contest* so badly that they'd try to spook out the competition? Maybe I hadn't been the only one to receive a warning note. I'd deliberated about whether to ask Florence or Hamish if they'd received one too––but if they hadn't, then I didn't want to alert the whole show that someone wanted me to quit. Or, even worse, what if they'd been the culprit? But I'd banished that thought from my head immediately. If I stopped trusting my friends on the show, then it really was a downward spiral from there.

I was supposed to be resting and baking, baking and resting. But each morning I awoke in a cold sweat. Did someone really have it in for me, or was I in real danger?

The only antidote I could think of was to repeat master baker and my witch mentor Elspeth Peach's protection spell every evening before bed and then again in the morning as she'd instructed. I'd stand before my bedroom window, staring out at the silver light of the moon or the beginning of a new day and recite the spell.

A chill went down my spine every time I finished.

A week had passed since we'd filmed the last episode. I'd scored a new design job that meant I could keep paying my mortgage. Even though my background was in graphic design, I also had a portfolio that cataloged some of my sketches. I'd put it online with my other work more because it pleased me than anything else. So I was thrilled that I'd been commissioned to illustrate a new hardback book about the English country garden. The publisher was famous for its beautifully designed books, and I was buzzing at the prospect of drawing trees, flowers, and herbs. I knew that Broomewode Farm would be the perfect place to begin.

I arrived at the inn a day early and checked in—my cat Gateau in tow, obviously—hoping to see Eve, who ran the pub and was a sister witch. But she wasn't due on shift until the lunchtime rush, so I'd have to wait for a gossip.

My new job wasn't the only reason that I wanted an extra day here before the baking show began filming. I also wanted to check on Susan Bentley and see how she was coping after the tragic death of her husband. So taking a stroll up to Broomewode Farm would be a case of killing two birds with one stone, so to speak. And the cherry on the top would be seeing Sly, Susan's Border Collie. I'd bought him a new red ball and I couldn't wait to hear the joyful bark as he went bounding after it. I'd left Gateau at the inn happily napping on the bed.

It was a gorgeous May morning, and as I headed up to Broomewode Farm, my sketchbook and Sly's ball in my bag, I thought about family. For so long, I'd been fixated on finding my birth parents, who'd abandoned newborn me in an apple crate for a reason that was still a mystery to me. But I was slowly realizing that the idea of family wasn't fixed. It came in many forms. I was more sure than ever that my birth parents could still be out there somewhere, and my drive to find them hadn't diminished. But now I had a new kind of family, too, my witch's coven. And after we'd been through so much together, even the other baking contestants were beginning to feel like family. The same went for Gina Philpott, my best friend and hair and makeup artist on the show.

Now that we were into May, the two hundred or so acres of fields surrounding Broomewode Farm looked more luscious than ever. The rolling green fields were vibrant; the flowerbeds on either side of the path had gorgeous blooms tumbling from the rich soil. I loved the variety of flowers that had been planted: vivid pink azaleas, their delicate petals a symbol of gentleness and femininity; sunshine yellow freesias, with their long stems graced by strange but beautiful knots of flowers; multicolor pansies, bluebells clustered in shady spots. I particularly liked the puffy round heads of allium. They reminded me of brightly colored cotton wool balls. There were also some early buds of foxgloves, beginning to bloom into elegant heads of white and purple. I stopped to pull my sketchbook from my tote bag and began to draw, enjoying the morning sun as it warmed my bare arms.

When I'd finished, I stood again, tucking my white T-shirt back into the waistband of my stonewashed jeans, and pushed on toward the farm. Soon, I saw the huge barn with its curved roof and the Somerset stone of the farmhouse. I heard the now familiar shift from crunch to silence as the path switched out wood chips for stone and the flowerbeds changed to laurel hedging and bright springy fern. I could smell Susan's amazing herb garden before I saw it, the fragrant and earthy scent tickling my nose and making me long for an herby cheese omelette. I guess my version of *it's five o'clock somewhere* was *it's lunchtime somewhere, right?*

But my hunger was curbed by the loud sound of a very happy woof. Sly burst from the side of the farmhouse and ran toward me, a blur of black and white fur. He leapt up, pawing my jeans, wagging his tail and barking. I laughed. "Hello, boy," I said, peeling his muddy paws away from my light pants. "I've missed you, my canine guardian angel, even if you are a bit mucky." I took the new red ball from my bag, and the very moment he saw it, Sly bounced up and down like an adorable maniac.

I lobbed the ball as far as I could (sports has never been my thing), and he bounded after it. In a flash he was back again, panting. I laughed. "Where's your mommy, hey?" He blinked, pink tongue still lolling, in crouch position, alert only to the ball. I threw it again and then went in search of Susan.

After trying the main house, I found her working in the barn, a huge array of herbs spread in front of her across a wide oak table with tree stumps for legs. Susan herself was perched on a smaller stump, singing something in a low, soulful voice that I couldn't quite catch. I was surprised she hadn't heard me calling out for her.

"Knock, knock," I said with a smile, lightly tapping the side of the open barn door.

Susan looked up. She was wearing a large apron over a

loose, white linen shirt. Her short, curling hair was pulled away from her face with a navy headband. Although she still looked pale, her eyes were more lively than they'd been when I last saw her. I hoped that meant she was getting some good rest and not worrying about how she was going to manage the farm.

"Poppy," she said, smiling. "What a nice surprise." She motioned to the stump next to her. "Come, take a seat. We can chat, and perhaps you wouldn't mind giving me a hand with all these herbs. I'm somewhat behind all my chores..." She trailed off.

I nodded and sat beside her. The table smelled absolutely incredible; all of earth's green treasures were in piles before me. Susan was an excellent herbalist.

I picked up a bundle of dark green rosemary and held it to my nose. Maybe I should think about making savory scones in tomorrow's first challenge. Rosemary and local cheddar. What would that be like?

"I use most of these in my tonics," Susan explained. "My mother and my grandmother before her were both herbalists, and they passed down their knowledge to me. Each herb has its own healing property, and if you blend them in the right combinations, then their properties blossom and multiply." As she spoke, her voice was tender, as if she was speaking about her babies. I guess they were, in a way. She touched the plants lightly, letting her fingers ruffle the green foliage.

"I tie these into bundles," she said, gesturing at a ball of string that I knew Gateau would go crazy for. "And then hang them from the line here." She looked up at a washing-line strung from the barn's rafters. "Once they're dry, I crush the herbs in my pestle and mortar and blend them into tonics with distillates."

"How do you remember which plant or flower does what?" I asked, shaking my head. "There's so many here, the combinations must be endless."

Susan smiled. "It takes time and patience, but I was also born into the herbal world."

"I'd love to learn even half, no––a quarter of what you know. After Elspeth cured Hamish's cold during filming last time, I've seen firsthand how powerful a tonic can be."

"*And* a little magic," Susan added.

"Of course," I replied.

Susan showed me how many herbs to tie in a bundle, and we set to work. I noticed that she had a small pile of foxglove, just like I'd seen earlier, except hers were in full bloom. "Don't foxgloves usually bloom later in the summer?" I asked.

"That's right. But there's a patch in the garden where they're sheltered. And I've been giving some special attention to these little beauties and got them to flower earlier than usual."

I touched the gorgeous trumpet-like petals, admiring how they hung toward the ground, their intricate patterns and pink hue. I explained my new illustration commission to Susan, who seemed thrilled. "Would you mind if I sketched these quickly?" I asked her. "I don't think I'll get another chance to see them up close for at least a month."

Susan encouraged me, and I took my sketchbook and charcoal pencil from my bag and laid it on the table, brushing away a few stray leaves and stalks.

"Foxglove is a devious flower," Susan said, somehow both

watching me draw and continuing to tie plants and flowers into bundles. "It has the ability to both cure and kill."

What? I so did *not* need any talk of killing this weekend.

I must have looked shocked, because Susan nodded. "It's true. Part of the plant is used in a prescription drug for congestive heart failure. Digitalis lanata, it's called. It strengthens the heart muscles and changes the heart rate. Foxglove is poisonous if you don't know what you're doing."

I stared at the beautiful stems in wonder. How could something so lovely and fragile be used both to keep hearts beating and to make them stop?

I enjoyed letting my pencil roam around the page and made a few shadings until the first outline was finished. I asked Susan if the tonics she made were seasonal, and she said yes. She talked me through the various tonics she only made in the late spring. She had some finished tonics stocked on shelves behind her.

"This one has valerian and lavender for those who suffer from anxiety. This is for increased energy. The chaste berry in this one helps women conceive."

"Wow," I said. I had zero clue plants could help with all that.

"But the mind is also powerful. Sometimes, simply believing a tonic will help is a big part of the effect. The power of positive thinking."

We worked in silence for a while, and I realized that we hadn't heard a peep out of Sly. He must be enjoying his new ball. I was trying to think of a way to tactfully ask Susan how she was feeling since Arnold's passing when she started to speak. "What's tomorrow's baking challenge? It's week three now, so the competition must be getting more intense."

I told Susan that this was the week of the scone. I was especially nervous of the scone challenge. It was such a perennially British bake. Although Norton St. Philip felt like home to me, after the age of eight, all my childhood memories were of the States. And treat-wise, that meant cookies, pancakes and red velvet cupcakes. I mean, I didn't even taste my first scone until I was in my twenties. I imagined that the rest of the bakers had been chowing down on those delicious suckers from the moment their teeth came through. And as if that wasn't enough of an advantage, Jonathon first shot to fame because of his tasty scones. It was his signature bake. He was going to be tough on us, for sure. Even more than usual.

Susan leaned across the table and began bundling up some rosemary. "Don't worry. You'll be brilliant. Are you going to play around with the recipe?"

"Well, I started doing batches made with cranberry and white chocolate. But something about that combo just wasn't working. I think it was too sweet." In fact, Mildred, my cottage ghost, had been outraged by my suggested flavor combination. When it came to scones, she was a stickler for tradition. But I wasn't about to tell Susan that––I was still getting used to the idea that I didn't have to hide my little gift. For now, it could just stay between Elspeth and me.

"So after a lot, I mean *a lot,* of panicking, I started making them with crystallized ginger and white chocolate. But I'm still not sure, to be honest."

"Sounds wonderful."

"It's inspired by some of the pastries I ate on a trip to Denmark."

Susan told me she'd be rooting for me tomorrow and

then gestured at the washing line above our heads. I stood to help her peg the plants so that they hung from their stems.

I touched her shoulder. "How are you getting on without Arnold? I mean, emotionally and physically." I grimaced. Why couldn't I find the right words? Gina, or Elspeth, probably Eve, too, would know exactly what to say and how to say it. I wished I had their way with words.

Susan shook her head. "It still feels so surreal. Like it all happened to someone else. It's hard to explain. But I've been lucky to have my sister here, although she's going home soon. The neighbors have been helpful too. I'm going to stay on the farm for the time being and hire some extra help for the big months. It's home now."

I told Susan I was happy to help in any way she needed: bees, herbs, or even a little sheep-shearing. She laughed, and it was good to hear that throaty guffaw. For someone who devoted so much time to healing other people with her tonics, it was tough knowing that time would be the best healer for Susan herself.

She turned away and I thought she was blinking back a tear. After a moment, she said, "Let me get you some eggs for your baking." She kept chickens and insisted that happy hens laid better tasting eggs. Since her hens were clearly happy, I was delighted to accept. In the world of the baking contest, who could say what difference an egg could make? She went into her kitchen and came out with a dozen eggs, which I carefully placed in my tote bag.

Together we finished hanging the bundles, and I was about to leave to get lunch at the inn when Reginald McMahan, the hobbyist blacksmith, appeared in the doorway.

Susan lit up. "Ah, Reg, how nice of you to swing by."

Reginald looked every bit the silver fox, just as he had the day I'd seen Susan leaving his cottage back when her husband had still been alive. His tall frame was clad in a loose, expensive-looking shirt that drew attention to his robust physique.

"Have you two been formally introduced?" Susan asked me.

I shook my head. Not formally, but I felt like I knew *a lot* about Reginald.

"In that case, let me do the honors. Reginald is a neighbor." She cleared her throat. "And a good friend," she added. "Poppy Wilkinson is one of the bakers."

He extended a hand and then shook mine with an almighty grip. *Whoa, cowboy, I'll be needing that wrist to stir with, thank you very much.*

"Pleasure to meet you properly, Poppy."

I tried to be cool, but I couldn't help feeling awkward. It had only been a week since Arnold died, and I couldn't shake the image of Reg and Susan looking pretty cozy on his cottage steps. But I didn't want to jump to conclusions. Or to judge.

"I saw your work in the estate gift shop, actually," I told Reginald. I was about to say how much I'd admired the fire tools, but I caught myself just in time. I'm sure no one wanted to be complimented on the tools they'd made that had been used as a murder weapon.

"Ah, yes, well, they won't be there for much longer. I'm not going to be stocked there anymore, so they're selling off what's left––at bargain prices."

I swallowed. Why did I have to mention the tools at all? What a doofus. But maybe now I could afford one if it was discounted enough. I'd love one of the pieces to hang beside my fireplace in the kitchen. Not a fire poker, though. I shivered.

I told Reginald how nice it was to meet him properly, and then I excused myself, feeling like three was definitely a crowd. Besides, what better way to celebrate my book contract than checking out the sale at the estate's gift shop?

CHAPTER 2

*A*fter throwing the ball a few more times for Sly, who pretended he didn't know what 'this is the last time' meant, I hitched my tote bag back onto my shoulder and set out toward the village. Sly kept running ahead and dropping the ball in my path until he finally gave up in defeat and turned back.

The sun was in full glory, showing off in the blue sky, and I tried to shake the weird feeling that had come over me when I witnessed how Susan glowed when Reginald entered the barn. I could see why she liked his company. He was certainly polite, and with that lovely head of bright silver hair and debonair manner, I supposed he was charming in his own way. But still. There was something about him I didn't trust. Was it his thin mouth, the way it was set in a stubborn line? I liked Susan a lot, but the friendship between those two was awfully warm when her husband had only been dead a week.

I shook away the thought and carried on walking back toward the pub. The big white tent sparkled in the sunshine, and the crew were already at work setting up. I headed that way, said hello to a couple of the crew I recognized and put my eggs and ginger and white chocolate chunks away.

It was crazy how familiar the tent felt when this was only week three.

It was nearly noon and I was drawn to the pub—and food, but the idea of getting a bargain on some of that lovely iron work was too appealing.

I had to pass the estate gift shop anyway on my way to the pub so I decided to stop in. The window display had changed. The fireplace tools were now gone and, in their place, Jonathon and Elspeth's cookbooks took center stage. Baking tins, *The Great British Baking Contest* aprons, and an array of wooden spoons and spatulas made a semicircle around them like a baking shrine. Some of the Somerset products were in the window, too: applesauce, fancy bottles of the local cider, dried apples, and cellophane packages of fudge, which I hadn't seen on my last visit.

The souvenirs for Broomewode Hall were next to the food goods. I felt a pang in my chest. I hadn't gotten anywhere near as far as I wanted with the search for my birth parents. There'd been so much drama, and perhaps I'd let myself get a bit waylaid. But as I looked at the tapestry of the great hall, I felt a renewed sense of urgency. This week I would make more progress. No excuses. It was time to turn my detective skills to where they were most needed: on my own trippy family history.

As I opened the door, a bell tinkled and the kindly-looking older woman who'd served me last week smiled up from a stool behind the till. "Hello again," she said. She lowered her silver-rimmed glasses to the edge of her nose and looked at me more inquisitively, a sparkle in her eyes. "The quince jelly baker."

Wow. I'd bought that jelly over a week ago. I told Eileen I was impressed with her memory.

"Nice to see you again," she said, extending a slender hand. It was mottled with age spots but soft to the touch, with a silver signet ring on the little finger. "And I can always match faces to what people have bought here. My gift for working in a gift shop." She gave a soft laugh.

I told her that the quince jelly had been delicious but today I was back to take a look at the fireplace tools. "I just saw Reginald, the blacksmith, over at Susan Bentley's. He told me that they were on sale."

Eileen raised an eyebrow at the mention of Susan Bentley but said nothing. I was suddenly shot through with guilt. Why had I felt the need to mention Susan's name? That was so thoughtless.

"Anyway," I continued hurriedly. "I have a cottage not so far from here, and it has a huge fireplace and hearth in the kitchen. I saw the tools last week and thought it would be fun to display some authentic hand-forged black iron tools at home."

"They really are lovely. I have an old cottage, too. I bought a pair of wrought iron candlesticks. They're lovely." She removed her glasses from the edge of her nose and let them dangle around her neck on a silver chain. She was wearing a pretty white lace shirt with a crocheted collar.

She was old. Her cottage was old. Maybe I should start my sleuthing here in the gift shop. "Have you lived here long?"

"Broomewode's always been my home. I'm lucky to live in such a beautiful village. Perhaps, at my age, it would be nice to be nearer a hospital, but except for some heart trouble, I'm in very good shape."

My own heart began to beat double quick. If Eileen had lived in the village all her life, maybe she knew the mysterious Valerie. "So you've always lived here?"

Eileen nodded. "My whole life."

I couldn't hold the question in any longer. "Did you by any chance know someone named Valerie who lived in the village more than twenty years ago? She might have worked at Broomewode Hall."

Eileen looked lost in deep thought, and then the lovely wrinkles in the corners of her lively eyes creased into a smile. "Yes, yes, I think I do remember a woman named Valerie. I used to be an occasional server at Broomewode Hall." She laughed softly. "Well, who wasn't? They've employed most everyone in the village at one time or another. Those were better days. The boom years. So much going on at the hall, parties and great galas. I can remember serving caviar on silver platters, coupettes of the finest champagne. The Earl and Countess were famous for their parties. I didn't know Valerie well, but I do remember her. She worked in the kitchen, I think. Why do you ask?"

I could have jumped up and down on the spot with joy but I tried to sound cool. "I think we're related. I've been trying to find out more about her while I'm in the village, but so far I've just hit dead ends."

She raised an eyebrow. "Really? I'm sure I must have a photograph of Valerie somewhere. I have a whole box of them taken during those years. I'd happily root through them for you if that'd be helpful?"

Before I could say thank you a million times over, the

shop bell tinkled and a woman walked in. She looked to be about the same age as Eileen and was wearing a lavender cardigan with a cream pleated skirt.

"Hello, Penelope," Eileen called out, smiling. "Come on through. Pop your things in the back, and then we'll start."

Penelope called out a hello in response and gave me a nod before disappearing through a door at the opposite end of the shop.

"That's Penny," Eileen said. "We've been friends since we were babies. She's just started here to lend a hand for the summer tourist season. I can't manage on my own, and two heads are better than one, I always say—even if they're two gray heads." She laughed softly. "Why don't you come for tea after my shift finishes? I'm done at two p.m., and then I'll try to find the photograph for you. Does four p.m. sound okay?"

I nodded eagerly, trying to contain my bubbling enthusiasm in case I came across like a total maniac, and thanked her profusely. Eileen wrote an address down on a piece of paper, and I tucked it into the front pocket of my jeans.

Penelope emerged from the back, and I went to check out the fireplace tools before I left. To my delight, they were half price. I chose a small wicker broom with a beautiful hand-forged iron handle. I smiled to myself. Although I had to keep being a witch to myself, I could hang a broom on my kitchen wall by the big fireplace like a private joke.

I took the broom to the counter, where Eileen and Penelope looked to be gossiping.

"Eileen tells me you're one of the bakers on the show. What a pleasure to meet you. You bakers are quite the celebrities in the village."

I blushed as she wrapped crinkly brown paper around

the broom. It was strange being a celebrity in this village. I was beginning to dread how crazy it would get when the show aired. "That's right. I'm very nervous for this week's challenge."

Eileen shot me a conspiratorial look. "Not that I know anything about this whatsoever," she said, "but if it did happen to be scone week, what with all these extra copies of Jonathon's book on scones arriving on Monday, then perhaps I might treat you to my own scone recipe later." She winked. "I've had eighty-odd years to perfect it."

I laughed and paid for the broom, taking a moment to flick through Jonathon's scone book. I'd caught him memorizing his own recipes and wondered if he'd have to do the same again before filming tomorrow.

I thanked both the women and left the shop with my broom. I looked at my watch. I'd have to wait another four hours before I was due at Eileen's and could see a photograph of the woman who might be my mother. Time couldn't go by fast enough till then. However, unpacking then lunch would help pass the time.

CHAPTER 3

*B*ack at the inn, I climbed the stairs to my room, still buzzing with excitement over my tea invitation and a chance to learn more about Valerie. None of the other contestants appeared to have checked in yet, so with any luck, I'd be able to get away later without having to make any excuses. I knew how Florence got when I went off on my "adventures," as she referred to them. And although they'd been nothing but supportive, I had a sneaking suspicion that Hamish and Gaurav thought I attracted drama.

I opened the door and had to swallow down my groan. Speaking of drama, there he was: my not-so-dearly-departed friend. I'd been hoping that maybe this week Gerry would have made it over to the other side.

"All right, Pops," Gerry said, giving me a mock salute. "I've missed ya. How you been?"

I had *not* missed Gerry's restless spirit, but I couldn't very well say so. Instead, I told him all about preparing for tomorrow's scone challenge, how I thought I'd perfected a crystallized ginger and white chocolate recipe. I scanned the room for Gateau but she'd gone out through the open window. Or maybe Gerry had hustled her out. There was no love lost between those two.

"I've got the perfect recipe for scones," Gerry said, "if you'd like some tips."

I rolled my eyes. What was it about scones that everyone thought they'd discovered the secret to the perfect bake? Before I could politely decline, Gerry launched into a scone monologue.

"Now, you'll find that the secret of good scones is not to handle them too much before baking and to make the mixture on the wet, sticky side."

He paused for effect, and I took the opportunity to butt in. "Yes," I said. "I've read Jonathon's book, too, you know."

Gerry looked offended. "These are my own tips."

"Yeah, yeah," I said, laughing. "That was almost word for word from Jonathon's book. In fact, I reckon you probably know them better than he does himself."

Gerry stuck out his lower lip and told me that there wasn't much else to do other than reading. "All this time to study for the perfect bake, but I can't grip a bloomin' wooden spoon. The irony."

Aww. I felt bad for Gerry. "Maybe you could help me decide on whether to stay traditional with my scone or experiment with something more exotic. I've been playing around with both all week, and I still can't make my mind up."

Gerry perked up. "Well, I'm glad you say that because I had a real light bulb idea this week." He paused and spread his hands open. "Imagine this: You're in Morocco—"

"I've never been to Morocco."

"I said, *imagine*, Pops. I know you have a good imagination."

I took a seat on the armchair and did my best to paste an attentive look across my face. It looked like I was going to be here for a while.

Gerry cleared his throat. "Right. Morocco. You're wandering through a souk, marveling at all of the merchant's wares. There are piles and piles of spices as high as they are wide, the most beautiful colors you've ever seen. We're talking sunset glory here, Pops—burnt orange, rich reds, golden hues. Saffron, coriander, paprika, ginger. Not to mention all those spices you've never even heard of."

Wow. I was seriously regretting indulging Gerry with this one.

"And then you come across the nuts and dried fruits," Gerry was saying, a wistful look in his eyes. "Stacks of them." He stopped, licked his lips, then looked me in the eye. "And that's when it all comes together. You update a British classic with the flavors of the East."

He tried to inhale for effect before realizing it wasn't possible. "Think of it. Scones made with saffron and dates, served with orange blossom jam."

He flopped dramatically back onto the bed, and I had to laugh. "Gerry, that does actually sound delicious."

"I could have won this round, I know it. But since I've been so rudely knocked out of the running, you're free to borrow from my genius."

"I just worry that Jonathon is such a purist. What if he only likes traditional scones?"

Just then a furry bundle leapt from the windowsill to the bed. Gerry shot up with a little cry.

"There you are, my sweet," I said to Gateau, who leapt from the bed to my arms and promptly began hissing at Gerry.

"Oof, that animal gives me the creeps," Gerry said.

I told Gerry off and put Gateau on the armchair where I'd been sitting. She curled herself into a tight ball, pointedly angling her backside in Gerry's direction.

I began to unpack my suitcase and let Gerry bore me with his fashion advice. I was secretly proud of my wardrobe choices for the weekend. Gina had helped me shop for some new shirts in a couple of boutiques in Bath last weekend, and we'd found some real gems. A cornflower-blue silk, a pistachio cotton with a lace trim. I was excited to pair them with my favorite jeans. And since the new season sales were on, I'd even splurged on a new denim skirt for the warmer weather. Gina had lent me a pair of her favorite earrings, too, gorgeous silver hoops with a line of tiny white shells swinging from the metal. If the baking this week didn't go my way, at least I'd look good doing it. Even Gerry had to compliment my choices.

"Wow, Pops. You're really moving away from the granny cardis and into some serious fashion."

I leaned over to pinch him for being so mean, but he just laughed as my hand passed through his arm. Gerry was so annoying sometimes it was hard to remember that he wasn't real.

But I was pulled out of my annoyance by the sound of Gateau hissing. Gerry was levitating, legs crossed, arms folded, from the bed to the ceiling.

"You've got to stop that in front of Gateau," I said, wagging a finger in Gerry's direction. "It upsets her."

He came down from the roof, muttering.

With my unpacking complete and a head full of new recipe ideas, I told Gerry I was going down to the bar to see Eve—and he was not allowed to follow.

"Aww, no fun," Gerry whined.

And then I had a bright idea. Annoying or not, Gerry had played the helpful sidekick during my detective work in Broomewode Village. The anonymous warning note I'd received last week was still nagging at me. Maybe he could do some secret ghostly scouting around the inn to see if he could find anything that looked to be written by the same hand. Or even with the same thick black ink.

Although this meant that I'd have to let Gerry in on another one of my secrets, at least I knew I could trust him: He had no one to tell.

I went to my tote bag and pulled out the note. I laid it flat on the desktop so Gerry could read it and explained how it had been left for me behind the bar downstairs. And that I was spooked.

Gerry read the note and said, "This is bad, Pops. There are some crazy things going on around here. It can be dangerous. Well, look at me. Dead!"

I didn't think anyone wanted me dead, just out of the competition for some reason. "Maybe you could help? I really want to know how serious this warning is or if it's a sick joke. I hate thinking it might be one of the other contestants, trying to scare me away, but after what Marcus was like with you..." I trailed off, as no explanation was necessary.

After the obligatory words of concern about my safety, Gerry's face lit up at the prospect of being useful. At least, I think his face lit up. Maybe it was more of a vibrating of his shadowy outline. "Yes, Pops! I'm your guy for the job! Anything but more haunting. I've been learning how to move things just with thought, so that could really be handy for this assignment. So far I've been having a lot of fun terrorizing the sous chef in the kitchen by moving his grater around the room, but this is way better."

He floated through the door. "Catch ya later, Pops."

I made a promise to myself that this week, as well as searching for Valerie, getting through to the next round and learning more about being a witch, I'd find a way to help Gerry move on from this world. Phew. I felt exhausted already.

Downstairs, the pub was buzzing with lunchtime business. The oak tables were crammed with guests drinking the local ales, and the smell of fish-and-chips tickled my nose. I went straight to Eve, who hadn't been there when I checked in earlier, and sat on a stool, waiting for her to finish serving a smart-looking businessman type.

"Poppy, love," Eve said. "It's so nice to see you."

The feeling was mutual. I liked Eve so much, and each time I saw her, she felt more and more of an older sister figure to me. Especially since I now knew she *was* one of my new sisters.

We caught up on each other's weeks, Eve filling me in on how busy the pub had been and all the village gossip, of course. Apparently, I wasn't the only person who'd noticed how much time Susan and Reginald had been spending with each other. "They came in for dinner together the other night. Tongues were wagging. And I did overhear Susan say that the earl has decreased her rent so that she can stay on at the farm. I like Susan a lot, but she's not going to make herself very popular around here if she's not more discreet."

Oh, dear. I hated hearing that Susan was the subject of gossip. I wanted to defend her against the rumors, but how could I when I'd been thinking the same thing myself? But it was also a relief to hear that things in the pub were carrying on as normal. I couldn't shake the feeling that things had started to go wrong in the village since I got there. What if I'd messed with Broomewode Hall's energy vortex by trying to trace my family? But I had to snap out of that thinking STAT. I admonished myself and told Eve that this week was scone week and I still hadn't decided on my final bake.

"Ooh, well, you're in luck. I happen to be in the possession of one of the most delicious scone recipes in all of Somerset."

I stifled a groan and listened as Eve imparted her scone wisdom, waiting for the moment I could butt in and order some fish-and-chips.

As she was talking, gesticulating wildly as if stirring a scone mixture in the air, I saw a familiar silhouette in the doorway. It was Benedict, Lord Winford, the handsome but snooty heir to Broomewode Hall and the earldom. As he came into the pub, he wasn't alone. A beautiful woman followed behind. She was wearing a silk wrap dress in burgundy and high heels in the same shade. She had a sheet of glossy blond hair, with impeccable honey highlights. Her brown doe-like eyes were thickly lashed, and she had the glow of the kind of year-round tan that suggested winters spent lying on the white sands in Barbados. She looked familiar, but I was having trouble placing her. Was she a model? Someone whose face I saw on magazines, pushing cosmetic miracles?

Benedict greeted Eve and to me, said, "Hello, Poppy. I hear you'll be baking scones tomorrow."

I couldn't help but roll my eyes. "Don't tell me. You have a secret family recipe for baking the perfect scone."

He frowned momentarily and looked taken aback. "I can't bake. Katie Donegal makes brilliant scones, but she's still in Ireland, I'm afraid. Anyway, you should really use your own recipes, not rely on other people's."

Argh, that man drove me mad. Before I could explain that I was being sarcastic, Benedict turned back to the beautiful woman. "Eve, Poppy, this is Ophelia."

I felt my eyes widen. Now I knew why she looked so familiar. This woman didn't sell cosmetics; she saved lives. It was Lady Ophelia Wren. She was a debutante and a doctor, famous for giving humanitarian medical aid all over the world. The press loved her, and she was often interviewed during medical crises in famines and war-torn regions. She was every woman's worst nightmare—drop-dead gorgeous *and* a selfless doctor, risking life and limb to travel to those who needed medical aid the most. I looked from her to Benedict and back to her again. Benedict was definitely punching above his weight there. I mean, what did he even *do* all day? Pose for portraits and mend the fences?

Lady Ophelia slipped her phone into an expensive-looking brown leather handbag. She politely ignored my gawping and extended her hand. Her nails were painted a gorgeous shade of pearlescent pink, and they caught the light as I took her delicate palm in mine. A gold charm bracelet jangled on her slender wrist.

"Pleasure to meet you," she said, in a butterscotch-rich voice that made me tremble a bit. Any good feelings I had about my own wardrobe for the weekend flew right out the window. How did a person manage to be that elegant and that intelligent? Surely it was unfair to be both. More surprising, she seemed nice.

"Shall we eat?" Benedict said, casually draping his arm around Lady Ophelia's shoulders. "I'm famished."

She looked up at Benedict, beaming with the adoration of a woman truly smitten. I supposed the two of them did make a handsome couple. Benedict was broad-shouldered and classically handsome if you like that kind of thing. Her blond hair was a lovely contrast to his dark locks, and each of them oozed that special brand of effortless elegance reserved for the very elite.

They excused themselves and left to sit at a corner table near the window. Very cozy.

Eve turned to me. "That's interesting. I thought those two broke up."

CHAPTER 4

$\mathcal{I}$ kept Eve company at the bar while I scarfed down a plate of perfect fish-and-chips. I'd been about to tell her about my chat with Eileen when I caught myself. Maybe it was silly, but after all the times I'd tried and failed to meet with Katie Donegal, I thought telling somebody about a possible link with the mysterious Valerie would jinx it. So instead I kissed Eve's cheeks as a goodbye, told her I was off for a walk (which was true) and that I'd be back later for dinner. It felt pretty glorious to be able to divide my day into when I was eating my next meal. I was trying to get as many calories in as I could so that I'd have the energy and stamina for a major bake tomorrow. Or at least that's what I told myself.

Outside, the afternoon sun was bright, with only a few cotton-wool clouds in the sky. The continued warm weather felt like a good omen. I set out for Eileen's, the inn's gravel path crunching underfoot. She'd written careful instructions on how to walk from the inn to her cottage and even drawn a simple map of the village.

According to Eileen's map, which had Broomewode Hall as a landmark, it would take me a good twenty minutes to walk from the inn to her cottage. I could drive in about five minutes but the walk would do me good.

With such gorgeous weather and the thought that I might be about to see a real photograph of my mother, my heart was already full and buzzing with anticipation. I was trying not to get overexcited, though. After so many false starts, I was wary that maybe Eileen wouldn't have the information that I needed either. I had to find a happy medium between being hopeful and being cautious. It was not going to be easy.

Following Eileen's map, I passed the residential streets that led to the shops around the village green. The lush grass was neatly trimmed and surrounded by flowerbeds full of purple hyacinths. I touched the amethyst necklace from Elspeth, grateful for the protection it gave me but also how I saw the beautiful purple color reflected in so many of nature's gifts. It still had that instant calming effect.

There was a small park by the green, and moms and dads with babies strapped to their chests pushed toddlers on swings. I watched one little girl chase a pigeon and then burst into tears as it flew away. The whole scene was so innocent, almost from another era.

When I arrived at Eileen's cottage, my jaw almost dropped, it was so pretty. It was set back from the road, with only two other cottages and a bungalow on either side. Looking at the cottage was like being transported to the eighteenth century. The roof was thatched, and the traditional brick, local to Somerset, had been painted white. Ivy crept across the left side until it tickled a lattice window. All the window frames had been painted bottle-green, and rambling pink roses framed the doorway, which was painted the same lovely hue as the windows.

The front garden was filled with traditional cottage flowers, beautiful plots of violets and primroses and some calendula and other herbs that I recognized from Susan's haul. The flowerbeds were divided by a pebbled path that led to the front door. Lilac and honeysuckle perfumed the air. Suspended at either side were hanging baskets with cascading multicolor spring flowers. The place looked like something out of an English home and garden magazine. Maybe it had even been featured. I made a mental note to train roses around the door to my own more humble cottage, the Olde Bakery.

The knocker was made of the same cast iron as I'd seen in the gift shop, but weathered, not polished. I lifted it, rapped on the door twice, and then stood back. I had to stop my feet from tapping in anticipation. To my right was a hand-painted sign with Plum Cottage written in a cursive script. What a lovely name.

Eileen opened the door wearing a floury blue apron over her lace shirt. Her white hair had strayed from its low bun, and her glasses were around her neck. "Ah Poppy," she said, almost as if she were surprised to see me. "Come in, come in."

Eileen ushered me into the narrow hallway, and we walked through a raised arch into one of the most lovely sitting rooms I'd ever seen. It was large, with plenty of sunlight flooding in through the windows, an old flagstone floor, open inglenook fireplace, and gorgeous wooden beams. The couches were upholstered in a floral brocade with plump cream cushions, and a dusky pink throw was draped along its back. She gestured for me to sit and said she'd be back in a moment with her famous scones. The room smelled of fresh-cut flowers, and I noticed she'd arranged fresh-cut roses into a silver bowl.

I couldn't sit. I was too excited. I paced by the fireplace. Among the array of porcelain ornaments arranged on the mantelpiece were the wrought iron candlesticks identical to the ones sold in the shop. Reginald's work really was incredible. Beside the candlesticks was a row of three silver-framed photographs. One was black and white and must have been Eileen in her youth. She was wearing a fifties two-piece skirt suit, and she sure was a looker.

Another of a small boy and a woman holding him had obviously been taken in a studio, eighties-style, with a marble-like blue backdrop. The third one was more recent. A man in his fifties, darkish hair with graying sides, had his arm around a woman about his own age on one side, and Eileen on his other. They were sitting at a garden table at the end of a long patio. Next to the photos was a vase of wildflowers, obviously picked from Eileen's garden.

And then I heard a tweet. And another. Was there a bird trapped in the chimney? I bent down and stuck my head into the fireplace to see.

"Goodness me, dear. What on earth are you doing down there?"

I shot up and hit my head. Ouch. I stood and rubbed the side of my head. Great, now I was a weirdo with a potential concussion—and I'd only been here two minutes.

I faced Eileen and rubbed the back of my head. "I think you have a bird trapped in the chimney."

She burst out laughing. "Turn around, my dear."

She pointed toward a nook by the front window, and my

eyes followed. And then I burst out laughing as well. In a huge gilded cage were two sweet budgerigars.

"That's Jimmy and Jenny. The cage is just for somewhere to put their feed. I keep the door open so that they can fly about wherever they like, but they mostly like to sit in the garden."

Eileen walked to the cage and made little kissy noises at the birds. Their green bodies seemingly puffed up with pleasure, and they bobbed their yellow heads back at Eileen.

"How do you tell them apart?" I asked.

"It's all in the nostrils. Jimmy here has bright blue markings, and Jenny's are white. But even without that, they sound completely different."

I raised an eyebrow. "Do they have a different tweet?"

Eileen gestured for me to sit, and this time I obeyed.

"Not so much tweet, as their voices. After a while, you can tell the difference. Sounds a little eccentric, I know. But it's true." She laughed softly and walked over to the cage and laid something on its floor. The budgerigars made a happy chirp. "I buy them cuttlefish bone from the fishmonger," Eileen explained. "They like to gnaw on it. Birds have wonderful personalities, and they're very chatty. Good company when you live alone."

I nodded politely. I did know what it was like to bond with animals. I just preferred the fluffy kind. Besides, my mind was racing with the hundred or so questions I had for Eileen about Valerie and how things worked at Broomewode Hall. But before I could let any tumble out of my mouth, Eileen jumped in.

"I'm sure you have questions for me, dear. Should we get started?" She checked her dainty wristwatch and took a seat on a lovely upholstered armchair across from me. "And please do help yourself to a scone. There's homemade strawberry jam and cream from Susan Bentley's farm."

Eileen had brought in a two-tiered serving set with four scones on the bottom and pots of clotted cream and strawberry jam on the top plate. It rested on a coffee table next to a china tea set, decorated with primroses. I accepted a little china plate from Eileen and happily took a scone and a dollop of cream and another of jam. Eileen poured the tea and then added a dash of milk to my cup. "It's whole milk," she said, "from a dairy farm nearby. Delicious."

I thanked her and took a sip of the sweet tea. She was right. Whole milk always made things taste wonderful.

Eileen sliced into her scone. "You see the secret to baking good scones..."

Oh, man, here we go. Buckle up for some more scone advice.

"...is to start with cold ingredients. Cold butter, cold eggs, cold cream. Believe me."

I nodded along politely, sipping my tea. Eileen meant well.

"And then you need to make the mix as cold as you possibly can before putting them into the oven. A quick blast in the freezer should do it. This way, they'll rise much better, and you'll get a lovely golden top."

I stole a quick glance at my scone. It looked pretty far away from golden. Positively anemic, in fact. But hey, I wasn't judging. Maybe my own bakes wouldn't turn out so grand either.

Eileen shifted on her chair and checked her watch again. She seemed distracted. If I wasn't going to have much time with Eileen, I'd have to milk her now for all the information I could get. Politely, of course. My heart began to pound. I spread some jam on my scone. "I was wondering if you managed to find any photographs of Valerie? I'm so curious to know as much as possible about her. No detail is too small."

Eileen looked out of the window. "Yes, Valerie. I've been trying to conjure her image to my mind."

She paused, and I took a bite of the scone. It tasted like chalk in my mouth. I tried to keep a pleasant expression on my face, but eating this scone was like chomping on the white cliffs of Dover. Had she forgotten an ingredient? Or added the wrong one? Like maybe some of that cuttlefish meant for the birds? It definitely hadn't bound properly. But the jam was sweet and delicious. I washed the dry mouthful down with my tea. Eileen continued to stare out of the window. She seemed to be miles away from the kindly, bubbly woman I'd spoken to in the shop. It was like she'd forgotten I was there. I cleared my throat.

Eileen looked at me and then started. "Yes, Valerie. She was a pretty young woman. A capable worker, if I remember correctly, if a little dreamy. Perhaps I'd even go so far as to say she was a bit of a romantic, her head in the clouds. She had a lovely manner about her. Kind and soft and you got well-wishing energy from her. She was happy enough serving all those la-di-da aristocracy during their galas."

If Valerie was my mom, then she sounded lovely. Except for the part where she put her own child in an apple box and dumped her in front of a bakery.

I pulled myself together. "So did Valerie work at Broome-wode Hall for a long time?"

"I can't quite remember how long for exactly. Katie

Donegal would remember. But she had a fall, poor love. She's in Ireland, I believe, visiting family."

"What do you remember?" I nudged her along. She seemed different from the woman in the shop. I wondered if she was overtired. Maybe working and then coming home to bake scones was too much for her.

"Broomewode Hall was home to lots of events in those days, so there was plenty of work. Not like now. Twenty years ago was a golden era for Broomewode Hall. The Champneys loved to throw the most elaborate parties, mostly for the young viscount and his friends. He loved life." She paused and shook her head sadly. "He died tragically young, you know. He had a terrible accident." She sighed and took a sip of tea. "Anyway, I would help in the kitchen for big events, and then lots of the villagers would get roped in for the bigger parties, as even then the Hall couldn't afford a full staff."

The birds flew out of their cage, over Eileen's head, and disappeared through the doorway. The movement seemed to shake Eileen from her reverie. "Let me get you that photograph," she said. "I found a box, and there's one of the staff outside on the lawns after a tea party. It's in the other room."

I nodded eagerly. Finally, this was it. I was going to see a photograph of the woman who might be my mom. My stomach fizzed, and I didn't think it was the chalky scone. I looked down at our plates (Eileen's clean, mine still full) and decided to ditch the evidence and be helpful by clearing away our tea things to the kitchen.

I called out that I was tidying up, but she'd gone upstairs and there was no response. Oh well, she'd find me. I walked into the kitchen and a big green Aga stove caught my eye. To me, the Aga was to ovens what the Rolls-Royce was to cars.

The kitchen was every bit as exquisite as the rest of the house. The windows looked out onto a beautiful garden, the lawns manicured and the flowerbeds just as busy and bright as they were in the front. The Aga emitted a pleasant warmth as I tossed my scone into the compost bin on the counter, and then carried the plates and cups to the giant porcelain sink.

The oak dining table was particularly eye-catching. The wood had been polished to really show off the natural grain and knots. I ran a finger over its surface. And then I noticed a stack of cookery books with an open letter sitting on top. The sight of a handwritten letter gave me a strange feeling in my belly, and I couldn't help but think back to that terrible warning I'd received. If only there had been some kind of clue in the handwriting––but it was all black capital letters. Not even one small thing that might betray the person who wrote it: no elongated P or wonky W. I shuddered.

I studied the handwriting of the letter on the table. It had a perfect sloping script, written with the kind of flowing blue ink that only comes from a fountain pen. I imagined that the person writing had been sitting at an antique desk, maybe even with an old inkwell carved into the wood. The letter was from someone named Oliver Jones, and the address was in Vancouver, Canada.

"Poppy!" Eileen said, her usually sweet voice sharp. "What on earth are you doing in here?"

I spun round. "Sorry, I was just trying to be helpful with the dishes." I gestured at the sink. *Definitely not snooping.*

Eileen held a shoebox in her hand. She glanced toward the letter, then at me. "I didn't mean to snap. It's just my angina. It flares up, and it's very uncomfortable." She smiled weakly. "It can make me somewhat of a grouch, I'm afraid."

Angina? My grandma on my dad's side had lived with angina for years, and I knew how painful and dangerous it could be. I looked into Eileen's kindly eyes and saw that she was worried. Her face was paler, too. I lightly touched her arm, and her wrist felt slender and fragile. "Do you have chest pain?" I asked her. "Shortness of breath? Shall I call an ambulance?"

Eileen shook her head. "No. If you'd just get me my pills, dear, and a glass of water. The pills are in the cabinet next to the sink."

I did as she asked, filling up a long glass of water and opening up her shaker cabinets to find an alarming array of pills, mostly supplements. Vitamin D, E, zinc, fish oil, castor oil. Her belly must be rattling! I riffled through the boxes until I saw a familiar brand.

"That's them, dear."

I handed her the pills and water, not sure how to properly express my concern for someone I'd just met.

I closed the cabinet and noticed a Van Gogh calendar on the wall. There was a black circle around the following Wednesday. Beneath, in a delicate script, black letters indicated a doctor's appointment and, later the same day, a line that said: *Thatcher and Gold, solicitor. One p.m.*

I swallowed hard. Was Eileen sicker than she let on? Seeing her doctor and her solicitor on the same day? Could she be getting her affairs in order?

$\mathscr{E}$ileen sat at the kitchen table and sipped her water. The shoebox was in front of her. She glanced at the open letter on top of the cookbooks and then reached over and folded the page with hands that shook.

"Forgive me. Today has been taxing. Things I haven't thought about in a long time." She paused and looked at me, her expression kind but weary. "Years go by so quickly. You can't imagine." She shook her head. "But we're here for a nice trip down memory lane, not a sad one." She pushed the letter under the cookbooks, then tapped the shoebox she'd brought in with her. "Here we are. Photos from the old days at Broomewode Hall."

Eileen smiled suddenly, and I realized my excitement must be plastered all over my face.

"It means a lot to you, doesn't it, seeing these photos."

She motioned for me to sit beside her at the old table, then she lifted the lid. Inside were several piles of glossy photographs, some so old they were curling at the edges.

"Every summer, the whole village used to be invited to

38

Broomewode Hall for a garden party. It was a huge event, a highlight of the year. Talk of what to wear went on for at least three months before." She paused and smiled wistfully. The sunlight streamed through the window and made a halo glow of her white hair. "Everyone dressed in their finest clothes."

She told me that this box had photos from the eighties and nineties. She riffled through, chose a photo and passed it to me, chuckling. "Though you'll see that the fashions of each era don't always hold up."

I took the photo eagerly from her hands and took the scene in greedily.

I recognized the lawns outside Broomewode Hall. A group of women surrounded a man, who I assumed was the viscount from his smart taupe linen suit and white linen shirt. I recognized Eileen immediately. Twenty-five years younger, she had light-golden-brown hair––and she was wearing a blue linen shift dress. A string of pearls hung around her neck, and she had her arm around Penelope, the woman I'd seen at the gift shop earlier, whose eyes squinted against the sun. I scanned the photo for someone who might resemble me. And then I felt my eyes drawn, as if by a force all of their own, to the figure of a woman.

"That's her," Eileen said, pointing. "On the other side of the viscount."

I exhaled. Finally. The mysterious Valerie.

In the picture she was laughing, frozen in time by the camera, mouth open and eyes crinkled. She was tall and slight, wearing a high-waisted patterned skirt and a pink halter-neck top. In her ears hung delicate drop earrings, though I couldn't make out the stone. She *did* look a bit like me around the mouth. And maybe the eyes too, but it was hard to tell with them so full of laughter.

As if she'd read my mind, Eileen leaned closer, stared at the photo and then back at my face. "You said there was a family connection? There's some resemblance, I think," she said softly, almost amazed. "The mouth."

I nodded. I couldn't bear to take my eyes away from the photo. I stared harder. Were her legs like mine? The slight tip of her waist? It was so difficult to tell in a group photo.

And then I saw something that made my mouth drop open.

It was the woman from the oil painting, the one I'd first seen when watching *The Great British Baking Contest* at home. In the photo, she was wearing the same shawl draped over her shoulder—the one just like my baby blanket! She wore a red dress with a sweetheart neckline and large ruby necklace. I peered closer. "Who is that?" I asked Eileen, pointing.

"That's the viscount's mother, the previous Lady Frome," Eileen said. "She was a glamorous soul. See the dress she's wearing? Princess Diana wore one very like it to the Royal Opera House that year."

"The viscount's mother," I repeated. Finally, I knew the identity of the woman in the oil painting. I couldn't believe my luck! The two women I was most curious about, in the same photo. "What can you tell me about the countess?"

Eileen shook her head. "Not very much, I'm afraid. She kept to herself when we were working in the house. But she was a kind lady. She made an effort to learn all our names and who our families were. She'd inquire after a sick aunt or remember a birthday. Her name was Elizabetta."

I repeated the name, half whispering.

Eileen took another sip of water. "We didn't know it then, but that was the last village party they ever had at Broome-wode Hall. The viscount was killed the following year."

I looked at that handsome man, so full of life, titled and rich. He must have thought he had the world by the tail, and yet he wouldn't live another year. And Valerie? What had happened to her?

"His mother lived until five years ago, but the truth is that when they buried her son, all the life went out of her. The old earl did his best. Brought his nephew in and tried to teach him how to run the estate, but he wasn't born to it, of course. The old earl died of cancer, though I always believed it was more that his heart was broken. His only son gone and his wife broken in spirit. She moved to the dower house, but she faded away. She was my age. So sad."

I asked Eileen if she had any more photos of Valerie, and we both went through all the photos in the box. There were a couple that showed Valerie in the background, one where she was handing the viscount a drink, but always she had her back to the camera or someone in the foreground obscured her. Still, I had one very clear photo, and I'd seen that shawl.

Eileen had been so incredibly helpful, taking the time to find the photos and welcoming me into her home. But I really wanted a close-up of Valerie, portrait-style, so that I could examine her face properly. It's hard to explain what it's like never having people around you that share your features. It sounds like a trivial thing, but there's great comfort to be taken from being able to actually see where you come from. I'd never had that before.

Eileen passed me another photo. "See the little boy there? That's my nephew, Timothy, my sister's boy."

I recognized the boy from the photo on the mantelpiece and told her so. She said the photograph next to it, of the older man and a woman, was the boy now grown up. "I don't see them so much these days," she said.

I sifted through the photographs of the garden party again, still hoping to catch another glimpse of Valerie. Everyone was clutching champagne coupettes or playing boules on the lawn. I looked at all the anonymous young men, dressed in their finest clothes. Could one of them be my dad? I had even fewer clues about him, but if Valerie was at this party, then maybe he was there too? I listened as Eileen talked to me about the village gossip: who ended up marrying each other, who later divorced. I studied the faces of the men, looking for the same kind of similarity I'd found with Valerie. I did this secretively, of course. As much as I liked Eileen, I didn't want to spill the beans about my witchy heritage to someone I'd just met. But I couldn't see any of my own features in the men pictured. Maybe my dad was from the next village over. Maybe it was a forbidden love. The Romeo and Juliet of Somerset.

As we delved deeper into the box, I could see how much fun those parties had been, how full of community spirit. I felt sad for the villagers now that these kinds of parties didn't exist anymore.

"It's been lovely, my dear, but I think I need to lie down." She trailed off and then glanced sideways at her watch, and I realized that it was time for me to make my exit. But now that I'd seen it, I didn't want to be parted from the photo. If I studied it a little longer, maybe it would provide me with the next steps to my search. I asked if I could borrow the photo, and Eileen told me I could have it. I promised to take good care of it as I slipped it into the pages of my sketchbook.

Then I told how her grateful I was for her time and for her sharing her treasure trove of photos with me.

"I'm more than happy to help, Poppy," she replied. "I'm sorry to cut our visit short, but I'm not feeling quite myself."

I made her promise to rest and to call me anytime she needed anything. Eileen walked me to the door. As we said our goodbyes, the late afternoon air was full of the scent of roses. On impulse, I asked if she'd mind if I sketched them and briefly explained about my project.

"Of course, my dear. It would be an honor. In fact, I'll give you some roses to take away with you. I have some I only picked this morning. I'll wrap them up for you. They'll cheer up your hotel room. And I'll pop in a copy of my scone recipe." As though this was a great treat and a surefire way to win the competition.

I didn't have the heart to tell this lovely woman that she'd be better using her scones as paving stones in the garden. I politely accepted the roses from her living room, wrapped in a damp paper towel and then a plastic bag. She'd obviously written the recipe out for me before I came, and that was affixed to the bag with a safety pin.

"I'm going to lie down, now, but stay as long as you like."

Eileen obviously loved gardening and had a green thumb. I quickly sketched the roses trained around the doorframe and then, taking her at her word, I explored her garden.

I could pretty much do all the sketches I needed in this one garden. Behind the house, she'd gone for English country garden style. Wildflowers mixed with peonies, and ivy climbed the old stone walls of the garden, which was deep. I wandered down a winding stone path, listening to happy bees at work in the many blooms. I did a rapid sketch of a fat bee bottom, the rest of its body inside a bright purple bloom I didn't know. I'd look it up when I got back to my computer. There were roses everywhere, and one in a quiet corner caught my eye. The blooms were a vivid pink, and the petals had the most exquisite shape.

I sat myself cross-legged on the lawn and settled my sketchbook on my knees, careful not to let the photograph fall out. The flowerbed was beautifully manicured––I guessed Eileen must employ some help. Next to the rose bush was a plaque, which I'd hoped would give me the name of the rose. But it was an inscription.

"To nurture a garden is to feed not just the body, but the soul."

I smiled. That sounded like something Eileen would say. I was sketching away, enjoying the moment, when I felt a sudden, cool breeze blow across my body. It made the hairs on my arms stand up. Maybe it was time I was getting back to the inn.

I pulled out the photo and looked again at the woman I thought was my mom. I turned the photo, twisting it this way and that, trying to see her from every possible angle. Eileen had written a date on the back. *Summer Fête, August 1994.*

I sat there, doing the math. My birthday was March 30, 1995. So on the day of the fête, my mom was either just pregnant with me or soon to be so. If Valerie was my mom, she got pregnant with me while she was working at Broomewode Hall. Did that mean my dad also worked at the house? My heart began to race. So many of the answers I was looking for seemed to be held in the manor house. I looked back at Eileen's beautiful cottage and hoped she'd be well enough for another visit soon. But what a success this visit had been. I was finally making progress.

CHAPTER 6

By the time I got back to the inn, it was six p.m., and suitcases lined the entrance. I could hear the now familiar voices floating out of the pub. I hung back and took a moment to collect my busy thoughts. I knew that the minute I walked through that door, the questions would come pouring in about my week and my baking. And if one more person today told me about their special scone recipe...

I took a deep breath and walked in.

"Poppy! There you are!" Florence called out gaily. She rushed over to me from the bar and kissed both my cheeks, Italian-style. "Texting is nice, but it's never the same as seeing someone in real life." She took a step back and appraised me with a serious look. I felt like I was on a makeover show, not a baking competition. "Fabulous," she said. "You look fabulous. Well rested, bright-eyed, and chic." She reached up and took a green leaf from my hair. "Nearly chic."

Florence herself looked more glamorous than ever. Her appearance always floored me because I didn't know how she did it. She was wearing a red silk wrap shirt, a long sheath of material tied around her waist in an extravagant bow, and a pair of wide-legged black trousers with delicate pleats that made the fabric ripple pleasantly as she moved. Her lips were the same glossy color as her shirt, and her reddish hair was raked back from her face in a high ponytail that had an enviable swish.

Florence dragged me over to the bar, where Eve was pouring a row of fresh orange juices and mixing them with sparkling water. If only I could talk to Eve in confidence. As much as I liked Florence and the other contestants, I wanted to keep my family life and my baking life separate. Not to mention my witch status. I took the sparkling orange juice gratefully and helped Florence carry the rest over to a table at the back of the pub where Maggie, Hamish, Gaurav and Priscilla were sitting. We weren't at what I'd come to think of as "our" table. When I asked, Gaurav told me that it had been reserved.

I passed out the drinks and gave everyone a hug before sitting down next to Maggie.

Gaurav talked about how strange it was going back to work in the time between filming. "It feels surreal. I'm back in my lab, continuing with the research I've been doing for years. Same building, same colleagues. But it also feels like I'm cheating on my baking life. Does that sound odd?"

I shook my head. I felt that way too. Being on the baking show was so all-consuming that regular life felt like a commercial break.

Priscilla nodded. "I've been feeling the same way at the salon," she said, describing how she felt as if she were just going through the motions of cutting and dyeing. As she talked, I admired how Priscilla's long, highlighted hair was piled atop of her head in an extravagant up-do that seemingly defied gravity. She always looked so flamboyant, and I liked that she always wore bright colors. She was very recognizable, and I suspected that when the show aired, she'd have a huge fan base of supporters.

"Being retired has its benefits," Maggie said, patting me on the arm. "I looked after the grandkids while my daughter was at work. And they didn't seem to mind me baking scones over and over again. In fact, I made them promise me they wouldn't tell their mummy how many they ate!"

We laughed, and all agreed our scone consumption had rocketed into the danger zone this week. Gaurav asked Maggie what kind of scone she'd settled on.

"I'm too old to learn new tricks," she said. "I've got to play to my strengths, and I've been making scones for fifty-odd years. If it isn't broke, then don't fix it, is what I always say."

Everyone nodded, but I could see from their faces that they were thinking the same thing as I was: Maggie was staking her turf. Now that we all knew she was sticking to the classic, what did that mean for the rest of us? Had anyone else made the same decision, and if so, would they really want to come up against Maggie in the competition? Practice definitely made perfect when it came to scones, and she had the monopoly on time. And if we were all deviating and experimenting with flavor combinations, would that mean each one of us would have to do something extra-special to make the grade?

"I'm sticking to what I know best as well, Maggie," Florence said. "I had my cousin send me chestnut flour from a deli in my family's home village to use for my Italian scone recipe." She laughed. "He had to seal it with several layers of bubble wrap to make sure it didn't explode along the way."

Hamish finished his juice and confessed that he'd had a disastrous week at work. Farm animals had been set loose on the Highlands, near where he lived, causing chaos and leaving him little time for baking practice, let alone looking after his own Shetland ponies. "I'm really worried I haven't practiced enough," Hamish said, looking downcast. "I don't want to be sent home yet."

Around us, the pub was filling up with the early dinner crowd. It looked like business was booming. Even though it wasn't yet dark, someone had lit candles along the windowsills and on the tables. The smells drifting out from the kitchen were delicious. I was about to suggest we order dinner without waiting for the remaining contestants to arrive (clearly my thoughts were with my stomach, not my social life) when a kind of buzz went around the dining room. For a second, voices lowered, and everyone looked at the entrance. In unison, our whole table turned toward the bar. It was the earl and his family––including Lady Ophelia. She was still wearing the dress I'd seen her in earlier but had put her hair up, and the result was positively flawless.

I felt myself flush as I remembered the last time I'd come face-to-face with Lord and Lady Frome, the way I'd been dismissed as "the help." Argh. And then I remembered how Lady Frome had frozen when I'd asked her about Valerie, as though even talking about servants in her presence was unacceptable. I lowered my head and hoped that I was too small fry for either of them to remember my face.

Lord Frome's voice boomed across the pub as he

announced his arrival to Eve at the bar. "And how's your family..." He paused for a split second.

"Eve," she whispered.

"Eve," the earl repeated loudly.

Oh, dear, what a show. Eve thanked the earl for asking and said they were all very well.

"Good, good," he replied and then ordered a bottle of champagne. "Is our usual table ready?"

Usual? Was he trying to make out that they had a preferred table they liked dining at? I'd never seen him in here before, and based on the reactions of everyone else in the dining room, it wasn't a regular thing. The old faker.

Eve nodded, and a waitress showed him to a large oak table in a more secluded nook of the pub, the one we usually sat at.

I turned to look at Florence. She was clearly enraptured, eyes wide, those perfectly glossed lips forming a little "O" of delight. She looked back at me and said, "Oh my goodness. That's Lady Ophelia Wren. I love her! A humanitarian and a fashion icon. She's such an inspiration. What on earth is she doing here among us mere mortals?"

Maggie nodded along, clearly an Ophelia fan, too. I explained that she was Benedict Champney's friend. I'd met her in the pub earlier.

"WHAT?!" Florence gawped at me. "You met Lady Ophelia Wren today and that wasn't the first thing you told us the minute you sat down? Tell me everything," she demanded.

I laughed and explained how it had been nothing, really. A chance encounter but that she'd been very nice. Much nicer than her boyfriend, in fact.

"Wow," Florence said. "I'm still surprised that the Champneys would choose to dine here though, among the rest of the villagers."

Hamish nudged her. "It's not the medieval times, Florence. Look at this lovely place. He's not exactly slumming it."

Hamish was right, but it *was* strange to see the Champneys at the pub, especially since Benedict and Ophelia had already eaten lunch here today.

A waiter who I hadn't seen before came to take our dinner order. I listened to him recite the specials—grilled cod and lentils with salsa verde sounded delish—and then gave the menu a quick scan. Eventually I settled on oven-roasted sea trout served with a hollandaise sauce and greens.

The baking chatter continued around me, but I was too distracted to really listen. The earl was making a big show of saying hello to each member of the inn's staff as they passed by his table, waving at some of the groundskeepers who were drinking pints at the bar. He'd obviously made an effort to "dress down," but his perfectly pressed red slacks and white shirt—even if the top two buttons were undone—looked stuffy.

Even Lady Frome was smiling at the staff. It certainly didn't match the image I'd taken away from my brief forays into Broomewode Hall. I'd been hustled out of there as if I was a door-to-door salesperson, trying to sell cat food to dog owners. That reminded me: I'd have to keep back a bit of fish as a treat for Gateau.

Florence was watching the new dinner group as though it were a play, which was what it looked like. The earl playing at being a regular guy who ate dinner in the pub, and Lady

Frome looking around her as though worried she might catch something if she sat on one of the pub chairs or dared to eat the food. Florence said, "I thought Benedict Champney and Lady Ophelia Wren had split. It was all over the papers."

Maggie leaned in closer and lowered her voice to a whisper. "Well, I read that although Lady Ophelia is titled, she rejects the whole aristocracy malarkey. With all the humanitarian work she does, she promotes the idea that everyone is equal. My guess is"—here her voice dropped another notch —"that the earl is bringing the family in here to show Ophelia that they're just normal folk."

I suspected she was right.

"It's probably time we had some wine, right, guys?" I said, realizing no one had ordered a bottle. "I'll go get us one from the bar."

The others thanked me, and I dashed over to see Eve.

"Sorry I've barely had time to say 'hello,' but we've royalty dining with us tonight," she said, rolling her eyes. "Once in a blue moon do the earl and Lady Frome come in, and it's a treat to watch him pretending he's a regular bloke who knows his people."

I leaned in because I enjoyed a gossip as much as anyone. "Maggie thinks he's trying to show Lady Ophelia that they treat everyone like equals." I nearly laughed just saying it. As if.

Eve got down six wine glasses from the rack above her. "I think she's right. Anti-snob or not, Lady Ophelia is from an excellent family, a real catch, and the earl is dying to get Benedict to marry her." She looked in the direction of the Champneys, her nose crinkling with delight. "And he is rather making a fool of himself. Look at him talking to poor old Stacey there. She's been a cook here for years, and he's never set eyes on the poor lass before, but now he's talking to her like she's his long-lost niece."

I strained to hear the conversation and managed to catch a snippet of the earl telling the poor woman how best to cook pheasant. Stacey looked mortified.

I turned back, and we talked about the weather forecast for the weekend while she uncorked the wine. It was going to be a nice weekend, though some rain was threatening for Sunday.

Eve set the wine and glasses on a tray, apologizing that she didn't have time to bring them to our table herself, when Benedict and his father came up to the bar.

Gaagh. One minute later and I would have missed them.

"Father," Benedict said, a cheeky look in his eye, "I think you've met Poppy Wilkinson. She's a baker on the show."

I stood frozen to the spot. Would he remember my face from the other week, when I'd canvassed at their door? I'd been so anxious to get inside the manor house that I'd pretended to be a movie location scout. What had I been thinking?

Lord Frome stuck out his hand. I briefly wondered whether he expected me to kiss it and then got ahold of myself and shook the offered palm.

But there was no need to worry. He showed zero sign of recognition. "How very charming," he said. "We're very supportive of the show, of course. Opening up our home to the cameras is a privilege. It allows us to share our heritage and history with the world."

Yeah, right.

He looked behind me and waved to the table of bakers who were staring at us. Not even pretending to play it cool.

"In fact, Eve, put that bottle of wine on my tab."

I thanked him, and before I could move, Lady Frome and Lady Ophelia joined us at the bar. Just my luck.

Unlike Lady Frome, Lady Ophelia looked happy to see me. "I'm so pleased you're here, Poppy. I'm such a fan of the show," she said. "I tape episodes and take them with me when I go on assignment. Especially if it's somewhere dangerous, where there's war or famine. I find the show really helps me to unwind and try to forget the troubling things I've witnessed during the day. It's my happy place."

Wow. I felt so not worthy.

"Would you mind if I went to say hello to the other bakers?" she asked.

She was asking *my* permission to speak to the bakers who were practically drooling just watching us over here. "Lady Ophelia, I'm sure they'd be thrilled to meet you."

She held up her hand and shook her head. "Just Ophelia. Please. I'd never use my title at all if it didn't help with TV ratings. Do you think starving children in war-torn countries care about some archaic patriarchal privilege?"

I shook my head, thinking this woman should run for prime minister. And Lord Frome, who wrapped himself in his archaic patriarchal privilege like a second skin, said, "Quite right."

Lady Frome was standing stiffly next to her husband. She wore a black high-necked top with a complicated-looking broach at the breast. Her body language was guarded, and I could tell she wasn't enjoying this little expedition to mingle with "the people." I could tell she'd recognized me, but Lady

Frome was too polite (or not interested enough) to let it be known.

"And has it always been your ambition to make cakes?" she asked me. Ouch. Her tone was so thick with a condescending air, I could have made it into a buttercream.

I smiled brightly. "It's a gift that came to me a little later in life. I'm a designer by trade, illustration and graphics."

"How wonderful," Ophelia said. Unlike the Fromes, she seemed genuinely interested in other people. "Not only are you an excellent baker but you're an artist. I so wish I could draw or even take a decent photo. I do so admire those with an artistic eye."

I checked for irony, but her expression was earnest. How could Lady Ophelia be so complimentary when she had such a selfless career, putting herself in harm's way to help people who needed it most?

I had a sudden, brilliant idea. If Lady Ophelia really did admire the arts, then maybe this was my way into the rooms of Broomewode Hall. I took a deep breath and tried my luck.

"Actually, I've been hired to sketch Tudor interiors for a home magazine." I swallowed. It was close to true, and if I did a good job with the gardens, maybe I'd be commissioned to do interiors next. "I've heard about what an excellent dining room you have at Broomewode Hall. I don't suppose you'd agree to let me sketch the room so that I can include it in my piece?"

I watched the earl squirm, his cheeks flushing slightly. His wife averted her eyes. But I knew that if he really wanted to show Lady Ophelia that the Champneys weren't snobs, he'd open up his home to a young artist.

"Of course, of course," the earl finally said after another

few seconds of obvious hesitation. "Whenever you like, Miss Wilkinson. But I don't suppose you'll have much time since your baking must come first." He chuckled a little to himself.

"Well, you know where the old house is," Benedict said with a wry grin.

Yes, I thought to myself, yes, I do know, and now I finally had an invitation to get inside that dining room.

"Excellent. I'll take the wine over to the bakers," Ophelia said.

Benedict didn't say anything, but he lifted the heavy tray before she reached it and motioned for her to go ahead.

I followed them back to the table with a warm glow in my belly. Safe inside my pants pocket was the photograph of Valerie. As soon as I could, I'd take a closer look at the painting of the woman who was wearing my shawl and see if it was an exact match for the one in the photograph. Or was there another explanation for the similarity?

Thanks to please-don't-call-me-Lady-I-never-use-my-title Ophelia, I now had a legitimate way inside Broomewode Hall.

CHAPTER 7

*T*he alarm clock jolted me from my dreams. Or should I say nightmares? All night long, I'd been tormented by strange visions of the long-dead viscount in riding gear and his mother in elaborate silk gowns and fine jewels, interspersed with images of horses galloping out of control, people laughing uncontrollably at parties, and the stomach-dropping sensation of falling from a cliff top. I'd woken in the night several times, stuck to the sheets in a cold sweat, and found Gateau watching over me from her position on the second pillow. Thank goodness for that cat. Just one stroke of her fur and I'd fall back to sleep.

But now I couldn't believe it was already time to get up. *And* bake! Today was the third week of *The Great British Baking Contest,* and if I wanted to win my place in the next round and stay in Broomewode Village, then I had better get myself straight and put my best whisk forward. If the last day or so had taught me anything, it was that *everyone* thought they could bake the best scone. The competition was going to be tough. Tougher than ever.

I dragged my sleepy self out of bed and into the shower, grateful that I'd already laid out my clothes for filming last night.

When I got out, Gateau was belly-up on the bed, lounging in a spot of sunshine. I stroked her soft fur and asked her to wish me luck today. She stared at me quizzically and then rolled onto her side so that I could scratch behind her ears.

I dressed quickly in my new cornflower-blue silk blouse and knee-length denim skirt. I paired the look with the shell hoops that Gina had lent me and finished it off with white running shoes. Maybe not the most stylish but good for standing on my feet all day and rushing from oven to fridge to work table. I appraised myself in the mirror, turning from side to side. Not bad, not bad. Now it was up to Gina to do her own kind of magic with hair and makeup.

I gave Gateau a final stroke, grabbed my tote bag of ingredients and bounded down the stairs for breakfast. I was going to need a big plate of food to get me through the day. Not to mention coffee.

Downstairs, breakfast was in full swing, and I spotted Euan, Amara, and Daniel, who all must have arrived late last night. I gave them a quick wave and then went to inspect the buffet. Not that I would ever admit to it in public, but the breakfast buffet was one of my favorite parts of being on the show. I heaped some fried mushrooms onto two slices of granary toast, added an egg, a local Somerset pork sausage and then a spoon of baked beans for good measure. A cup of steaming black coffee and an OJ, and then I could take on the day.

I slipped into a seat next to Hamish, and he asked me if I was nervous. I was. It was strange how that sinking feeling, like the morning of going back to school after the summer holidays, wasn't dissipating. If anything, the pressure was building, and it seemed that Hamish felt the same way.

"I expected to be voted out on the first show," Hamish confessed. "I really didn't think I had what it takes." He shook his head sadly. "It feels like blind luck that I'm still here."

I was surprised to hear Hamish second-guess his talents again. He was a wonderful baker and had lovely presentation skills. Plus, his experience as a police officer meant he had a great demeanor on-screen: confident but not showy, friendly but not a stuck-up, and he was excellent at explaining his process. I told him as much and he looked happier. He leaned closer, "And you're like that girl a bloke feels like he can talk to and the women all treat you like their best friend. The viewers will love you."

I knew he meant it as a compliment, but I was so the girl next door. I was the one men could talk to about women like Florence, who was the one every man wanted to be with.

Maggie and Gaurav joined us, but it appeared that I was the only one whose appetite didn't suffer with nerves. Maggie picked at a sliced grapefruit and toast, and Gaurav barely got his scrambled eggs down. As usual, Florence was last to breakfast, making an entrance in an emerald-green A-line skirt and ruffled white top. She grabbed a couple of banana and bran muffins from the basket, and then we walked to the grounds, the now familiar tent a luminous shade of white in the sunshine.

It was a chillier morning than yesterday but still lovely. Birds were tweeting, and the scent of hyacinths filled the air. Florence chattered inanely about her chestnut flour, pausing only to take bites of both her muffins, which she clutched in either hand. The chatting and the eating was a nervous habit I was used to by now, and I let the conversation wash over me as we drew nearer to the competition tent. My ears pricked up as I heard Gaurav tell Maggie he was making orange-chocolate-chip scones. What a unique combo.

As usual on the first morning of filming, the tent was buzzing with activity. The cameramen were setting up, the sound guy, Robbie, was testing mics. I dashed over to Gina, and we hugged. When I drew back, she was studying my face with a frown.

"I see someone didn't get any rest last night."

Trust Gina to get straight to the point. She ordered me to hop into the makeup chair.

"I did, but I had nightmares." I closed my eyes as Gina began to slap moisturizer onto my face. I told her about my horrible dreams about the viscount and his mother and all about my visit with Eileen. It felt so good to be able to talk freely about searching for my family. And Gina knew better than anyone else in the world what my new discoveries really meant to me. She was so excited for me, and I promised to show her the photograph after we'd finished the morning's bake. The stroke of a soft bronzer brush on my cheeks was soothing.

"There you go. Now you look a little more lively," Gina said, holding up a mirror. I grinned. Somehow she'd managed to make me appear as if I'd just returned from a long weekend in the South of France. The whites of my eyes popped, the circles beneath them banished. My lashes looked dark and thick, and I had a healthy glow from whatever wizardry Gina had enacted. She added a pink gloss to my lips and ran a brush through my long, dark hair then pulled it into a simple pony tail.

"Perfect," she said and then whispered into my ear, "Now go win this round."

I thanked her and rushed over to my workstation where Robbie was waiting to mic me up. Gerry had briefly returned last night and admonished me for not agreeing to try his recipe, but I'd come too far with my ginger and white chocolate concoction to follow the whim of a frustrated ghost. I'd asked him if he was getting anywhere with discovering who might have written that warning note but so far, nothing. I tried to keep up my hopes, though. If anyone could find me some answers, it would be a snooping spirit.

I lined up my equipment on the sparkling white surface and took a few deep breaths.

I glanced around the tent, intrigued to see what ingredients the rest of the contestants were using. I knew that Maggie was sticking to tradition, but she wasn't the only one. Daniel had announced he was sticking to the basics, too. I wondered how those two would fare, going head-to-head. I couldn't see what Amara was making or Priscilla, but Florence was doing a fruit-and-nut-style scone, with her special chestnut flour, currants, and pistachios. Euan had a medley of chocolate propped alongside his pack of caster sugar.

A familiar rush of nerves coursed through my body. I touched my amethyst necklace, hoping for a little magic to come through and make my scones a success. But as soon as I had the thought, I felt terrible. What was the one thing Elspeth had warned me not to do? Use magic for my own good. What if I had upset the magical world with my wish?

Oh man, Poppy, way to make myself feel worse. I hurriedly took the thought back. *To the powers that be. Ignore that wish from me. I've still a lot to learn. Your trust I wish to earn.*

Would that do it? I sincerely hoped so. I really needed more time to learn about being a witch. I'd always seen ghosts, which was no picnic, especially when they kept trying to get my attention, like Gerry, who'd floated up onto Florence's workstation and was jumping up and down on her special chestnut flour.

I had instinctive urges that had proved powerful, especially when fueled by strong emotion, but I had no structure to my magic. I wanted a file box like I had for recipes so I could call on the appropriate spell whenever I needed it.

And then it was lights, camera, action, and the two hosts, Jilly and Arty, came in, followed by Elspeth and Jonathon, who walked into the tent, arms linked and smiling.

Showtime.

Elspeth was wearing a floor-length plum skirt that sat high on the waist with a belt of the same color, a crisp white shirt tucked into its folds. She looked so elegant and poised, her eyes carefully lined and her cheeks flushed with just a hint of blush. Next to her, Jonathon looked the maverick in a loose blue shirt with dark jeans and a thick silver bracelet I'd never noticed before on his wrist.

Arty and Jilly did their usual warm-up banter. Arty turned to Jilly. "I hear the competition is fierce to create the perfect scone. Look at the bakers, ready for battle, determined to stake their claims to the baking crown and crush their opponents. Today's going to be bloody, Jilly. Not everyone will survive. We're calling this episode *Game of Scones.*"

We all laughed dutifully because we were here to enter-
tain the home viewers as well as trying to win the baking
contest.

But they weren't done. Jilly shook her head sorrowfully.
"Scones will roll. And you know what they say about a rolling
scone?" She looked at Artie.

He answered, "It gathers no mousse."

Oh, that was a groaner, but the corny schtick was part of
the fun of the show.

Jilly took over. "So, bakers, it's biscuit week and your first
challenge will be to craft the perfect scone. Jonathon, you
rode to fame on the back of a scone. Could you tell the bakers
here today a bit about what you're looking for in the perfect
bake?"

Jonathon drew himself up to his full height, as if
preparing himself for a difficult speech or, even weirder, as if
he had to defend his special scone recipe. "I happen to think
that my recipe will give you the best scone you'll ever make.
But I'm more than happy to be challenged by our bakers
today."

We all let out a nervous giggle. As if anyone would ever
dream of challenging Jonathon.

"For a traditional scone, it's all about the quality of your
basic ingredients. You want a nice crunch when you first bite
into it, and then the firm but moist crumb on the inside." He
paused and looked round the room, smiling a cheeky smile.
His blue eyes sparkled mischievously. "I have an outrageous
appetite for scones, so I can't wait to try everyone's take on
this classic. Will they play it safe and wow Elspeth and me
with an excellent rendition of the classic?"

Elspeth spoke up now. "Or will they play a wild card and

astonish us with some interesting and unusual flavor combinations?"

Jonathon paused and rubbed his hands together gleefully. "I can't wait to find out."

Elspeth smiled, obviously impressed with Jonathon's speech, though to my ear, he sounded a little stiff.

"Well, then, I think it's high time we put these bakers to the test," she said.

Jilly was wearing a leopard-print shirt-dress that was definitely eye-catching. "Contestants, best of luck to you all," she said. "You have one hour."

Arty was in tight black trousers and a purple paisley shirt. "On your marks, get set... Bake!"

And there was that familiar feeling. Legs like jelly. Stomach dropping. Sweat breaking out. *Get a grip, Poppy. You know the drill. You know the recipe. Now get the eggs and butter out of the fridge and get on with it.*

Wow. Turns out I have a pretty bossy inner voice.

I took my ingredients from the fridge and store cupboards and reached for my favorite mixing bowl. To my total horror, I could sense the cameras coming closer, and I knew that when I turned around, there would be Jonathon, ready to question my methods.

Why, oh why, did he have to pick me to terrorize first? I hadn't even started yet. But then I had a flashback to the other week, when I'd found Jonathon reciting lines from his own cookbook in the rose garden. He was human like the rest of us. I just had to remember that and keep my cool. And besides, Jilly and Arty had teamed up and were heading for poor Hamish. Maybe I'd get off lightly.

"Poppy," Jonathon began, "I can see you've got your basic

ingredients ready. Will you talk me through what your first steps are?"

I liked how Jonathon posed it as a question, as if I could say, *Actually, yeah, I do mind. Can you go ask someone else?*

"Sure, I'd be happy to," I replied, trying to grin through my nerves. "As you said earlier, the key to getting things off to the right start is to break down the butter and flour into a crumble-like mixture." I'd weighed out my ingredients and began mixing them with my hands. "Do you see how it's going lumpy? Well, that's a good thing in this case. Now I'm going to add my sugar, eggs, and baking powder and sort of *turn* the mixture, trying to incorporate the liquid into the flour."

I stopped my little monologue to actually concentrate on what I was doing. The last thing I wanted was to tell the people at home how to make a great scone and then mess up by not paying attention.

Jonathon peered into my bowl and made some ambiguous noises as I stirred. Was he encouraging me or just clearing his throat? I really didn't have a clue. But he made no signs of leaving me to it either. I guess witch-to-witch solidarity did not exist when it came to the show. Unless he was trying to telepathically improve my scone making.

I swallowed and continued my own practiced speech. "At this stage, it's time to start adding the milk. Just half to begin with. And see how I'm turning the mixture gently? It's all about being slow and thorough. There's no wiggle room for nerves here." I laughed at my own joke half-heartedly. "And then you add the rest of the milk."

Jonathon did a little whistle through his teeth. "That's an impressive technique, Poppy. You're sure to get the inside of the scones nice and soft and fluffy like that. I'd love to stay and find out if you're adding your own twist to this recipe, but we should move on. I'll have to wait till the taste test."

Phew. Music to my ears.

I thanked Jonathon and then turned my focus to the next step.

It was time to add my white chocolate chunks and crystallized ginger, both of which I'd bought from the tiny organic store near my cottage. The chocolate was the creamiest white chocolate I'd ever tasted, not overly sweet like so many brands, and real vanilla pods lent it a rich and layered texture. Pairing it with tiny chunks of crystallized stem ginger gave the whole mix an amazing fiery sweetness, with just the right amount of depth. Or so I hoped.

I sprinkled some of my remaining flour on my work surface, tipped the soft dough out, and then used my hands to fold the dough until it became smooth. I had to be careful not to overwork it.

I stole a quick look at the rest of the contestants. Jilly and Elspeth were talking to Euan, who was talking about chocolate. Everyone else had their head down, working with real concentration. We all seemed to be at the same stage. No dramas. No mess-ups. Not great TV drama, but on this side of the camera it was such a relief. Soon I saw the cameras turn to Maggie, who was about to start rolling out her dough. She showed Jilly her recipe and laughed her comfortable grandmother's laugh. "Look at my recipe. It's so old the paper's going yellow. But I've been baking this recipe since my mother first taught me. Tried and true it is and that's what I'm hoping Jonathon and Elspeth will like."

I heard a buzzing in my ears and could barely breathe.

Okay, she wasn't super close, but when she held up her recipe for the camera I could see the neat block printing. Exactly like that on the note telling me to go home.

Could grandmotherly Maggie be trying to terrify the other contestants? I couldn't believe it. Didn't want to believe it. I had to put my suspicions out of my mind for now and get on with my baking.

The final stages of the scone challenge went by in a flash. I used my special pastry cutter to stamp out the scone rounds from the pastry, and then I prepared my special glaze. To give my scones a sweet, crunch topping, I brushed a little milk over the top of each scone, then dipped it into a shallow plate of demerara sugar before carefully placing it on the baking tray. And that was it. I'd done everything I could do make these perfect. It was up to the oven to do its thing.

Fifteen minutes passed, and I washed up and added some fine shavings of white chocolate to a ramekin of clotted cream. I'd planned to serve my scones with a little pot of homemade ginger marmalade, but I was worried that Jonathon was such a purist, he'd hate the deviation from traditional jams. But I spooned a little out anyway. Better to be ambitious, I figured. And confident. And then hope that no one noticed you were faking it.

When the scones were golden, I took them from the oven and placed half a dozen of the best-looking treats on a pretty amber glass plate I'd found in a charity shop. I breathed a huge sigh of relief. They looked lovely, but the real test would be in the taste.

The timer clanged, and Arty ordered us to stop what we were doing.

I joined the rest of the contestants as we made our way, trembling, to the judging table.

I surveyed the scene. Each plate of scones looked delightful. The basic shape was the same for everybody, but the colors and embellishments varied from person to person, and I could really see how each of us had put our own stamp on the recipe. It seemed as though everyone had baked to perfection. But they had to taste as good as they looked. And if the last couple of days in Broomewode Village had taught me anything, it was that everyone and their dog thought that they knew the secret to the perfect scone.

I held my breath as Jonathon and Elspeth took turns slicing the scones in half and examining their texture. But despite being famous for his scones, Jonathon kept stealing sideways glances at Elspeth to see if she approved of each bake. Was he having a confidence crisis? It didn't make sense. But my thoughts didn't linger on Jonathon for much longer, as soon it was my turn to be judged.

I watched Elspeth spread my clotted cream with white chocolate shavings onto the still-warm scone and spoon a minimal amount of ginger marmalade on top. I gulped. Had I gone too far with the marmalade business?

I watched as they both took a modest bite...and then turned pink as Jonathon said it was delicious. "Moist, but with a good crumb, spicy from the ginger but sweet from the chocolate. I'm sold," he said. I beamed.

But Elspeth was less convinced. "There's some excellent baking here, that can't be denied. But for me, there's a little too much ginger in the scone mix. That being said, the white chocolate is a perfect pairing, and I can't fault the scone base itself. But your ginger is a little overpowering."

They moved on, and I tried not to feel like I'd failed Elspeth. *Stop being so sensitive, Poppy.*

I tuned out of the rest of the judging, too concerned about whether I'd just blown my chance to spend another week with my new coven and continue searching for my family with the aid of my new friend Eileen.

So it was to my surprise that suddenly I saw everyone clapping Florence on the back. Had she won with her fruit and nut scone? From the theatrical curtsey she was now taking, I could only assume: yes. Wow. I felt kind of bad about how surprised I was. I hadn't really taken her love of chestnut flour seriously, but it had obviously been impressive. I joined with the congratulations, happy just knowing how ecstatic this would make Florence. Maggie came second with her perfect, traditional bake. I would have been happy for her but I had my suspicions she wasn't quite as genuine as she appeared. I was pleased when Hamish came third. He'd used buttermilk in his scones and claimed it was a Scottish tradition. He'd gone savory instead of sweet with a cheese and dill combination. I was hoping to get a taste of his scones before the crew scarfed up all the goodies. Poor Daniel came in last. Both Elspeth and Jonathon had agreed his traditional scone was dry and lacking flavor.

I came fifth, which was good enough for me. My ginger had overpowered my recipe but not my chances. I'd take that as a win.

After cleanup, it was time for lunch. I couldn't face the canteen-style tent lunch with the cast and crew. I needed to get away. I decided to clear my head with a walk before the next round. Maybe I'd even have lunch with Eve in the pub.

Gerry appeared beside me and I'd never been more

happy to see my annoying ghost of a friend. "Fifth isn't bad," he said, obviously misunderstanding my mood. "Not saying Moroccan influences wouldn't have given you the win..." Though he obviously thought I'd been a fool not to use his recipe.

Quickly I told him about Maggie's recipe and how I suspected she might have written the note. He was ready to believe I was being sabotaged by another contestant. Well, it had happened to him!

"I'll search her room, Pops," he told me. "Don't worry. If she's behind this underhanded ploy to get rid of you, she'll be exposed. You can count on me."

His ability to pass through doors was a real bonus where snooping was concerned. "Check all the rooms. See if anyone else has a note like mine."

"Would they bring them back to the inn?"

I looked over at him. "I did."

Reginald McMahan was coming out of the gift shop and directly in my path. I told Gerry to vamoose and he did, turning backflips past—make that through—Reginald.

And there was Sly, bounding toward me from the path that led to Susan Bentley's farm.

"Hello, boy!" I said, bending down to give Sly a friendly pat. "Good to see you."

A man came from the same path, a stranger, carrying Sly's slobbery red ball in his hand. He was young, maybe early twenties, with a tuft of reddish-blond hair, and was wearing gardening clothes. He emitted a kind of buzzy energy.

Sly immediately abandoned me and went into crouch mode, ready to chase that ball. "You want this, do you?" the guy said, with a northern accent I couldn't quite place.

Then he lobbed the ball across the field and Sly was off.

"Poppy, how did you make out this morning?" Reginald asked, reaching us.

Elspeth didn't like my scone, I came in the bottom half and I suspected a fellow contestant of sabotage. Not the best morning. But, I didn't want to sound churlish, so I told him that it'd been fine but I hadn't won the round. I watched Sly leap in the air for the ball and catch it in his mouth. I could learn a lot from Sly about focus and sticking to a goal.

Reginald said, "I really should have given you my mother's scone recipe. It's a winner."

"Oh, you don't even know what a good scone is until you try my granny's," the stranger piped up. "Cold hands. That's the secret. And she puts everything in the bowl, and everything in the fridge before she starts."

Would family scone recipes follow me around for the rest of my life?

"Poppy, this is Edward," Reginald said. "He's a new gardener at Broomewode Hall."

I gave him my best smile––any employee of Broomewode Hall was a friend of mine––and we chatted for a few minutes, then I excused myself. If I was going to have any stamina for this afternoon's baking, then I'd have to get some lunch into my belly.

CHAPTER 8

*J*checked my watch; I only had forty minutes before I was due back at the tent, so I tried out a light jog to get me there faster. Hopefully no one would see me attempting to be sporty. Denim skirts were not made for getting anywhere fast.

But meeting the new gardener for the grounds had me thinking about my (somewhat forced) invitation from the earl to visit Broomewode Hall. I was itching to get inside as soon as I could. And then my mind went whirling back to Eileen's box of photographs, especially the one she'd let me keep of Valerie, which was now safely tucked inside my recipe folder. I'd been so excited to get it, I hadn't even asked Eileen to name everyone in the photograph, and now I was kicking myself. What if they still lived in the village like Penny and Eileen? Actually, why hadn't I asked Eileen if Penny would talk to me, too? I'd let myself get carried away and hadn't made the most of my time with the elderly villager.

But I also knew it wasn't just me. Eileen had been distracted even before her angina started playing up. Maybe

I'd caught her on a bad day. I'd go back to the gift shop after filming today and bring the photo with me. Since Katie Donegal seemed to be sequestered in Ireland, maybe Eileen could help me compile a list of people who could potentially help trace my genealogy. Plus, maybe I could ask to see the box of photos again and this time hunt for men who might be my dad. Might Eileen remember who Valerie spent her time with that summer? Should I tell her more about why I was asking all these nosy questions?

But then I thought about that warning note. Did I really think Maggie would stoop so low? No. Something wasn't right in Broomewode, and I didn't want to put a nice old woman like Eileen in any danger. I'd keep my guess that Valerie might be my mother secret for now.

The sun was in its noontime glory, and I felt my cheeks flush pink under its warmth. Despite being preoccupied with the Valerie mystery, I never got tired of being in Broomewode's beautiful grounds. I picked up my slow-jog pace and rounded the corner to run the short distance on the roadway to the inn's entrance. I was running, and the sun was in my eyes, but I swear it was out of nowhere that a car appeared, going way too fast and headed right for me.

In that instant that I realized I was in danger, I threw my hands out and yelled, "Stop!"

I felt the power come from my hands, pushing, pushing against the speeding vehicle. Even as my heart was pounding, there was a terrific screech of rubber on asphalt as the silver car jerked to a stop, only narrowly avoiding running me down.

The car's driver glared at me through the window, as if it was my fault he was driving like a maniac. I stared back in shock, and we locked eyes as I slowly dropped my hands. The man looked vaguely familiar, mid-fifties, hair graying at the sides, but I couldn't place him. And then, just like that, he roared past me, following the road around the pub.

I stared at the retreating car. How could someone almost run a person over and then not even stop to check that they were okay?

I wiped the dust from my lovely new denim skirt and scowled as the car disappeared from view. It had all happened so fast, I hadn't even thought to check the plate number.

I looked down at my hands, still tingling slightly. Maybe I wasn't very good at spells yet, but there was some serious power in these hands.

INSIDE THE PUB, it was busy. All the tables were full, and everyone was tucking into huge plates of food, and sipping on beers and wine. It had been so long since I'd had a proper weekend, with no work and no baking, that I could hardly remember what leisure time felt like. I promised myself that as soon as I was through with the show, I'd make some time to slow down. Go for long walks through the beautiful Somerset countryside, see friends and start baking for fun. Life was too short.

I headed straight for Eve at the bar, and my expression must have said it all, because she rushed through an order of roast beef and horseradish baguette, poured me a refreshing pint of sparkling water with elderflower cordial, and then commanded me to sit.

With a heavy heart, I told her that not only had my scones failed to impress Elspeth this morning, I'd almost been run over by some awful man with zero manners. I described him: about fifty, graying hair, red cheeks, in a silver car. I didn't catch the make.

"Did you see someone like that just in here?" I asked. "They came out of the inn's car park."

Eve looked puzzled and shook her head so that her long braid flopped from side to side. "Look around. Loads of men in here fit that description. Between the locals, film crew and weekenders, it could be half the people in here. But you weren't hurt?"

"No." I glanced around to make sure we wouldn't be overheard. "I put my hands up and yelled 'stop,' and I think my magic saved me."

"Good girl. Follow your instincts. Your magic's powerful. I can feel it."

"I wish it was powerful enough for me to drag that guy back and give him a piece of my mind."

My sandwich arrived. I checked my watch. I only had thirty minutes left before I was due back at the tent. I sipped water, and between bites of the delicious sandwich, I told Eve that I'd had tea with Eileen Poole yesterday and that she'd given me a photo of Valerie. Eve asked me to fetch the photo so she could take a look.

I knew Eve had only been in Broomewode for a few years, but maybe she might recognize someone who'd attended those legendary garden parties. After missing a golden opportunity to ask Eileen yesterday, right now I needed all the help I could get. I ran up to my room for the photo.

When I returned and showed her, Eve's kind eyes crinkled as she smiled. "Look at the corner table over there." I followed Eve's finger as she pointed and saw an older gentleman and woman lunching. They both looked pretty bored and weren't even speaking as they ate.

"That's Bill Morrison. I'm sure that's him in the photo there. Him and his wife, though they were a lot younger then."

I squinted at the photo and then back at the couple. It was them all right. What luck! I hesitated to interrupt a complete stranger's lunch with a photograph of them from over twenty years ago. But I had to make it back to the tent in time for filming. Also, it didn't look like I was interrupting much.

The woman was immersed in something on her phone, and the man was staring out the window.

I walked over to their table and cleared my throat, and they both looked up. I introduced myself, apologizing for interrupting their lunch, and explained that I was tracing my family history at Broomewode Hall and wondered if they could tell me more about the garden parties.

The man looked delighted. "Of course, sit down, sit down." He gestured at a stool. "I'm Bill Morrison, and this is my wife, Barbara."

Barbara smiled and put down her phone. "We'd be happy to help, if we can." She touched a bottle of rosé that was bobbing in an ice bucket. "Could we offer you a glass?"

I would have killed for a cool glass of rosé, but I still had to bake this afternoon. I thanked her and sadly declined. "You're one of the bakers. We were watching for a while this morning. It's so exciting, isn't it?" And before I had to remind them about the nondisclosure agreement, she shook her head and laughed at herself. "And very good for business in the village. Brings in lots of tourists. Well, we'll watch for you specially when the show airs. Now, how can we help you?"

I took out the photograph and put it on the table. Bill studied it and laughed.

"Look at me with all that hair. And you, Barbara, look how slim you were back then."

Barbara's smile slid from her face. "And look at you, staring at that pretty young waitress."

My heart beat double quick. She was talking about Valerie. Now was my chance.

"Did you know the young waitress?" I asked, trying not to hold my breath.

They both shook their head. And then Bill said, "She wasn't here long. I remember that she had a lovely laugh."

Barbara's head snapped up, and she glared at her husband.

"A lovely laugh?" I asked, hoping for more information.

"Yes, it was a proper belly laugh. You could hear it across the lawn," Bill replied.

"Do you remember anything else about her?" I tried again.

But Bill shook his head again.

I tried not to look disappointed. They were both still staring fondly at the photograph.

"There's Eileen, of course," Bill said. "She runs the gift shop, you know. Never married. Shame. The rumor was that she had a soft spot for the Jones boy. What was his name?"

His wife closed her eyes. "Oliver." She took a sip of rosé and then sighed.

"That's it. I was only a boy myself when he went missing."

"Missing?" I asked, intrigued. If they couldn't tell me

about Valerie, who was also missing from Broomewode's collective memory, then maybe there might be a link with this Oliver guy.

"Yes. He disappeared. Back in the sixties, I believe," Bill said.

His wife corrected him. "It was the fifties, not the sixties, Bill. I remember because he was fifteen years old, the same age as my eldest brother, Graham. Oliver ran away from home. It was a sad, sad business."

Bill took up the tale. "It was in all the papers. The police conducted a search right across the county. There was talk of murder, kidnapping, witchcraft and all sorts."

"Witchcraft?" I felt an uncomfortable tightening across my chest. I hoped no one had witnessed my little speeding-car-stopping stunt earlier.

"Aye. It was a more superstitious time."

"I remember being afraid of all the police cars," Barbara said. "Frightened that a child could go missing. There were people out day and night, searching. But they never found a hint of him. No clues. The whole village was in despair."

Bill nodded. "But then there was the letter."

"The letter?" I asked, literally on the edge of my seat now.

"Yes, one day a letter arrived for his parents. It'd been sent from Canada. He wrote that he'd run away because he was unhappy at home and bullied at school. He'd ended up making friends with a Canadian and had gone back there with him, where he'd stayed."

Wow. That had to be a hard letter for his parents to read. What had happened in that household to make a fifteen-year-old boy want to leave? Wait. A letter from Canada? I'd seen one of those just yesterday.

"His sister still lives in the village. Penelope."

Oliver Jones was the name written at the top of Eileen's letter. And he'd written from Vancouver, Canada.

"That's Penelope Jones, there," Bill said, pointing at the photograph again where Penny was standing with her arm around Eileen. "That's his sister. Ooh, those two used to fight like little maniacs. Close they were, but dreadfully competitive. I remember seeing them run races through the village or challenge each other to duels." He shook his head. "Such a sad thing. She missed him terribly when he was gone."

Barbara said, "She went to visit him once. But the parents were too old to travel by then. He wrote them every so often, but he's never come back. It broke his parents' hearts." She paused and shook her head sadly. "And Eileen's, I've always thought. She was sweet on him." Barbara leaned in. "That's why we all thought she never married."

I decided to keep Eileen's most recent letter to myself. I didn't want to stir up any more village gossip. Maybe she was enjoying a long-distance love affair with her childhood friend. And why shouldn't she enjoy it in privacy?

I thanked Bill and Barbara, and they told me they'd come and watch some of the afternoon taping.

I checked my watch and realized I was going to have to sprint it back to the tent. But this time, I'd be on the lookout for any crazy drivers. I was going to need my toes intact to stand up and bake, thanks very much!

CHAPTER 9

"And where on earth have you been?" Florence demanded, giving me a sulky face. "I won, and my favorite person on set wasn't even here to have a celebratory lunch with me." She flicked her red hair over her shoulders.

"Oh, Florence, I'm so sorry." I paused. I needed some kind of white lie to get me out of this one. "I had to run back to the pub to feed Gateau because I forgot to give her breakfast this morning." I touched the amethyst around my neck and hoped that it would protect me from any consequences of a white lie. "And then I saw Eve and ended up eating at the bar. Forgive me. I'll make it up to you later, I promise. We'll do something lovely in the evening to celebrate properly."

She frowned at me. "Honestly, Poppy, you are so mysterious sometimes. It's like you have another job or something."

Hmm. She'd kind of hit the nail on the head. Looking for my family *was* like having another full-time job. Now I had to get myself together and bake on national TV for millions of viewers. But after my wobble with the scones this morning, my near brush with death, and new information about

Broomewode Village, my head could not have been more out of the game.

"Poppy?" Florence said, breaking me out of my worry bubble. "Are you okay? You seem a bit frazzled."

I relayed my awful incident with the crazy driver and said it had shaken me up.

Immediately Florence pulled me into a hug. She smelled divine, and I was already regretting my "light jog" earlier. "Aw, you should have said. I've been in two car crashes myself, and I'm so nervy on the roads now. You must be spooked." She pulled away and then slipped an arm around my shoulder. "I'm sorry I was cross. Let's get you straight to Gina."

By the time Gina had fixed my makeup and hair and I'd had a chance to calm down and catch my breath,

I was the last to reach my workstation. Everyone else was ready to go, and I got a few raised eyebrows from Hamish and Gaurav. I hoped that they didn't think I was off playing detective again. Although come to think of it, I was, but I was trying to be the detective who solved the mystery of my own life story.

I hurriedly prepped my station, and then Florence returned to hers just in time for Fiona, the director, to announce that the technical challenge would begin filming in one minute.

As part of biscuit week, our technical challenge was to make brandy snaps. And I was worried. Biscuits really weren't my thing (I was definitely more of a sponge kind of girl).

The sound guy, Robbie Denton, rushed over with a mic. He'd trimmed his full beard since last filming and now looked more like someone in their early twenties. "Where have you been? You should have been back ten minutes ago," he admonished me.

Oh, man, I'd upset everyone today.

"Sorry," I whispered.

He clipped my mic and adjusted the wires before running off set.

Jilly and Arty came into the tent first. I wondered if the two of them were keeping up their flirtation. Jilly must have been ten or maybe even fifteen years older than Arty, but perhaps their shared love of comedy was enough of a bond?

Maybe I just didn't understand enough about romance. It had been a while since my last boyfriend, and I truly enjoyed living in my own place, doing things on my own terms, so much so that I hadn't given any thought to dating lately. Gina was always going out on dates; nothing thrilled her more than spending hours swiping left and right, choosing the perfect outfit, curling her hair, putting on "her face," as she called it. But I'd rather take a long hike through the countryside than go to a fancy bar and drink cocktails. And romance seemed like a lot of heartache. Just take Eileen and the missing boy Oliver, for example. If what Bill and Barbara had told me was true, Eileen never got over her first love.

The two celebrity judges came in next, and Jilly announced that our technical challenge was to bake a brandy snap. "Is this a tricky technical challenge for our bakers?" Arty asked Elspeth.

"Oh yes," replied Elspeth. "It may appear to be simple, but there are hurdles that each baker will have to overcome. First is getting the right consistency, dissolving the sugar correctly, and then spacing them properly on the tray to bake will play a big part in their success. It's tricky, but I think they're fun, too."

Fun? Who was Elspeth trying to kid here?

"I like brandy as much as the next bloke," Arty chimed in. "And I might have got snapped once or twice."

Brandy Snaps was not good news. I'd made them before but usually burned them so my confidence was pretty low. The problem with brandy snaps was that they were supposed to be light, super-sweet, and crunchy—not too brittle and not too soft. It was a tricky balance. And then you had to get the cream filling the perfect consistency.

I could tell he was about to do the countdown so we could begin. I hoped this challenge went smoothly and I managed not to burn the biscuits. With luck, we'd be finished in time for me to pop up to Broomewode Hall and remind the earl that he'd promised I could sketch his dining room. I really wanted to do it while Ophelia was in residence so he wouldn't give me the brush-off.

"Pops!" It was Gerry, sitting on my workstation and waving his hands in front of my face. In a frantic tone, he said, "Stop staring into space and get baking."

I looked around the tent and saw that we'd been given the go-ahead and everyone else was dutifully weighing out ingredients. I had to snap out of this mood and into brandy snaps! The time restriction was going to be one of the hardest factors in this challenge, and I was already behind.

"Thanks, Gerry," I said softly.

"It's not Maggie," he told me. "Tell you more later, but I read her diary. She thinks you're lovely. And her block printing doesn't match the writing on the note. FYI, she's not so keen on Florence, though. Thinks she's two-faced."

"Later," I whispered, though I was relieved to know Maggie hadn't tried to sabotage me. Some good news, at least. I thought she'd been a bit harsh about Florence but reminded me she'd written in the privacy of her own diary and I should try and forget what I'd heard.

I weighed my butter and demerara sugar and combined them in a pan so that the sugar sat on top of the butter. My panic began to subside. Maybe I was getting over myself. But then I realized why I suddenly felt calm: Elspeth was looking at me, and I could tell she'd sensed my mental upheaval and was calming me down.

I weighed out my golden syrup and put the pan onto the stove. I knew the mix had to dissolve slowly, otherwise the sugar and butter would crystalize and become gritty. I stirred gently, trying to banish non-baking thoughts from my mind. But all I could think about were Eileen's photographs and my plan to get into Broomewode Hall.

I suddenly felt a rush of electric energy. It was Elspeth, her delicate hand momentarily touching my shoulder. I looked up, and her face was full of concern. She lowered her voice. "I can't be seen to be checking up on you, but I'm worried. Is everything okay? You look pale and agitated."

"Oh, Elspeth. I can't focus." I wanted to tell her everything, about the car nearly running me down and the picture, but I'd have to wait.

Elspeth was about to reply when Jonathon joined us. He gave Elspeth a very stern look that I couldn't understand. But Elspeth obviously did. She immediately changed tone, praised my stirring technique, and glided away to speak to Daniel, who was being followed by the cameras as he panicked about whether he'd added too much sugar.

"Smells good, Poppy," Jonathon said and then joined Elspeth.

I looked down at my pan and realized that the heat was far too high. I groaned and turned it down, hoping that I hadn't already done irreparable damage. It should take fifteen minutes to melt everything down in a smooth and glossy liquid, and I really didn't have time to start again.

I stirred and stirred, staring into the pan like it might have some answers for me. Once the mix was dissolved, I had to let it cool for a couple of minutes.

The rest of the bakers were already adding their remaining ingredients. I really was behind. My heartbeat sped up, and I started to get that horrible queasy feeling that rolls through your body when the dread begins to trickle in. I'd known going into this afternoon's filming that I had to bring my A game after the scones. But what had I done instead? Gone on a hunt for information about my family and got my emotions all fired up.

"Bakers, you should be getting ready to get those brandy snaps into the oven," Jilly announced. "Hurry up and make it snappy!"

I quickly sieved the flour and ginger into the mix. But the mix was still too warm, and I had trouble making it combine properly. I forced myself to wait a couple more minutes. And, of course, that was when Arty decided to return to my station.

"I see you're running a bit behind the others," he said.

Er, yes, thanks for stating the obvious.

"A little, yes," I said through a forced grin. "But now I'm ready to add the lemon juice." I poured it in and then got a piece of baking parchment ready.

"So next you're going to spoon out the mix?"

Thanks, Arty. He was stealing my lines.

"That's right. I'm only going to put four dollops on each tray. Otherwise they might run into each other."

Arty snorted. "Exactly the kind of technique I need to employ with my ex-girlfriends."

I laughed, but I was worried. As I spooned the mix, I could see it wasn't glossy or smooth enough. Either the sugar hadn't dissolved properly, or I'd added the flour too soon. I felt tears prick the corners of my eyes. But no way was I going to start bawling on TV. I knew that the comedians lived for these kind of meltdown moments. I had to get it together before Arty noticed I was on the brink of panic. I swallowed down my emotions and faked a smile at Arty. Thankfully, he had no idea that my mix was all wrong––he was here for the jokes, not the bakes, so he simply wished me luck and moved off with the cameras.

I went through the rest of the steps like a woman possessed, got the brandy snaps into the oven, and said a little wish-you-well prayer with way more urgency than usual.

When the biscuits had spread out across the parchment and had the appearance of a sheet of lace, I took them out. At least they weren't burned. I'd oiled the handles of several spoons, ready to roll the snaps into the right shape. I was beyond grateful that I hadn't burned the batch. Now this was the tricky bit. I had to roll them all around the handle while they were still soft, otherwise they'd harden, and then gently press the edges so that they made a cigar shape. Once my tray was finished, I left them there while I tackled the cream filling.

The cream needed to be thick and light but not too stiff. I

knew from past experience that it was easy to over-whip the cream. Then I filled a piping bag, twisted the top, and piped the cream into the hard snaps. But now they were cool, I could see that the biscuits didn't have that glossy sheen they needed. I'd poured the flour into the mix too quickly. But there was no time for regrets now. Elspeth sounded the clangor, and I placed the rest of the biscuits onto my decorative china plate.

My stomach dropped into my shoes as I walked over to the judging table. These snaps were nowhere near my usual standard.

I stole furtive glances at the other plates. They all looked pretty much the same, but on one plate, the cream was dribbling out of the biscuit. I studied the faces of the other contestants and immediately saw that the oozing biscuits belonged to Priscilla. Her usual jolly expression had soured, and worry lines were etched across her forehead. Poor Priscilla. She hadn't whipped her cream to a thick enough consistency. I felt for her; it could happen to anyone. But right now I was more worried about myself. Mine looked all right, but was the taste okay?

I braced myself as Jonathon and Elspeth did the taste test. I winced after each crunch, waiting for the moment they got to mine. And when I was finally put out of my misery, I held my breath as Elspeth delivered her verdict.

"The biscuit has a good snap to it, and the cream is the perfect consistency. I like this snap a lot, even though it might be a little sweeter than strictly necessary. Perhaps the sugar hadn't quite dissolved enough early on. Even so, I'd say this was a pretty good brandy snap."

What a relief.

Hamish was crowned the king of the brandy snap, and Priscilla was urged to keep on top of her cream whipping if she wanted to do better next time, as she came in last. I came in fifth again. It wasn't the bottom, but I really needed to do better. Daniel was seventh, so he looked even more worried than I was.

There was a round of congratulations for Hamish and then a multitude of hugs given to Priscilla, who was far from her usual loud, outgoing self. I felt for her, but after a consolatory hug, I headed out. I really wanted to get to Broomewode Hall tonight so that maybe tomorrow I could actually be focused enough to smash the showstopper challenge.

I was not ready to be sent home. Not when answers seemed to be within my grasp.

CHAPTER 10

While I'd been frantically baking I hadn't even noticed that the weather had chilled. Silvery gray clouds now covered the blue, the sun just a distant yellow haze behind them. I shivered in my light shirt and wished I'd thought to pack a cardigan in my bag today from the wide selection I had brought with me. Between the ovens and the stress, I was usually plenty warm in the tent, but the walk back to the inn could be chilly.

I crossed the freshly mowed lawn. The flowerbeds had recently been watered, and the air smelled earthy and fresh. Edward, the new gardener, must really be on top of his game. And who did I find scratching up against a bayberry bush but Gateau?

"Where have you been roaming, little one?" I asked. She looked up at me, as if to say *I had important cat stuff to do, okay?* I let her finish her scratch and then bent down to take her into my arms. "Come on, we've got some very pressing detective work to be getting on with."

Gateau meowed softly, and I took that as an indication she was game.

"And we'll have to be super quick. After today's disappointing results, there's no way I can afford to be distracted tomorrow." I paused, aware that I was talking out loud to a cat but also finding her to be the perfect sidekick.

Silence from Gateau. Oh well. Was she not impressed with my plan?

"Okay, I guess I'll have to try and wing it. You just concentrate on looking adorable."

Gateau licked a paw in response.

"Perfect," I said, smiling.

I was nearly past the gift shop when I decided to pop in and see if Eileen could answer a few of the questions I'd forgotten to ask yesterday. Like who else was in that photo. I glanced at my watch. Perfect. There were twenty minutes before it was due to close. As I opened the door, I had a brief but clear memory of helping out at the Philpotts' bakery when Gina and I were kids. Although come to think of it, we'd only counted the one-pence pieces in the till float and then "helpfully" gobbled up the few mini apple turnovers that were left on the counter.

I reminded myself, not for the first time, that I did have family. If I found out about my birth mother and maybe father, that would be great, but I mustn't lose sight of the way the Philpotts and my mom and dad had raised me.

The bell tinkled charmingly as I pushed open the door, Gateau trotting in beside me. Eileen was beside the till, perched on an antique stool. She was wearing a maroon corduroy dress, and next to the rich color, her face looked very pale. I stepped closer and saw that her eyes were also rimmed red, and blue shadows sat beneath them. Had she been crying? Or was it something worse?

"Eileen?" I said, rushing over to the till. "Is everything all right? You really don't look well. Is your angina playing up again?"

Eileen glanced at me with a blank look on her face and then rearranged her features to a brighter expression. "Oh, Poppy, I'm fine, just miles away."

But she didn't look fine. Not one bit. I wished she would tell me what was plaguing her; she had the same distracted air as when we had tea together yesterday, but this time there was something distressed about it, too. I touched her slender hand. She felt ice-cold.

"What can I do for you?" Eileen asked in a faint voice. "How did the baking go today?" She suddenly coughed, a deep, breathy, chest-racking sound, and I went round the side of the till.

"Eileen," I said with a stern voice, "It's obvious you're not well. Let me call you a doctor." It was more a command than a question.

"No, no. I think I need to lie down," Eileen said quietly, catching her breath. "Would you mind awfully helping me to close the shop?"

"Of course. Don't you move," I said. "I'll do it all, then I'll drive you home. You need to rest."

She nodded, and I could see she was relieved.

"Shall I start with the till? Talk me through the cash-up." The cash register was an old model, a relic from the sixties probably, and I fiddled with the clunky buttons. Eileen didn't answer, and when I glanced over, she'd stood and was swaying.

I ran forward and caught her as she fainted, then I eased her down to the floor, my arms shaking with the effort of lowering her slowly so she didn't hurt herself.

Gateau raced over and sat by Eileen's side.

I crouched beside her, checking her pulse. "Eileen?" I said. "Can you hear me?"

Silence. I managed to find her pulse. But it was very faint.

Gateau looked up at me as if to say, *Do something!*

Right, Poppy, get it together. I needed help. And fast. I pulled out my phone, but the reception was terrible in this stone building.

I rushed out of the shop, wondering how long it would take an ambulance to get here. I was about to punch in 999 when I saw a familiar figure striding toward the tent. It was Benedict Champney. Of course, Lady Ophelia was a doctor. She was much closer than the local ambulance.

I called to him, and I must have sounded as frantic as I felt for he broke into a sprint, concern etched across his face. "Poppy, what's happened?"

"Where's your girlfriend?"

"She's not my girl--"

"I need a doctor. Now! It's Eileen."

Benedict looked behind me into the gift shop and saw Eileen lying in a heap on the floor. "Right. You stay with Eileen. I'll get Ophelia. She was making a phone call outside the inn."

He took off at a run, and I went back inside the shop. Poor Eileen looked so frail and helpless on the floor. I looked around and scanned the shop's shelves until my eyes fell on a pile of those beautiful embroidered cushions I'd so coveted last week.

I took out the softest, most plump-looking cushion and carefully slipped it under Eileen's head. She struggled to open her eyes, her expression one of bewilderment. I grasped her hand. It felt so tiny, and still—so icy cold. "Eileen, I'm right here with you. Just concentrate on your breathing. Try to breathe as deeply as you can. Help is on the way."

Gateau meowed and nuzzled against Eileen's side.

She turned the corners of her mouth up slightly, as if she was trying to give me a weak smile, but I could see that she was shivering.

I darted around the shop again and found a thick woolen throw, made for cozying up on a couch. Perfect. I draped the throw over her, tucking it around her body and under her chin. "Is that better?" I asked.

But instead of answering me, Eileen lifted her feeble hand and clutched my wrist. She was desperately trying to tell me something. I leaned down, putting my ear to her face so that I could hear what she had to say.

"The letter," she whispered, struggling for breath. "Key is the frog. Must...so sorry."

And then Eileen let out a gasp of air, and her eyes fluttered shut.

"Please don't go," I said, but while I held her cold hand, I saw her spirit leave her body and float upward.

As much as I didn't want to believe it, Eileen had breathed her last.

CHAPTER 11

I sat beside Eileen's body for what seemed to be hours, holding her hand, as if I was waiting for her to finish her last sentence. In fact, I was desperate to know the end of what she was trying to tell me. But when I heard the door chime again, I realized that only a couple of minutes had passed. I looked up, and Lady Ophelia Wren rushed toward me, Benedict a few paces behind.

Ophelia knelt beside me.

"Her name is Eileen?" Lady Ophelia asked, very efficient.

I nodded, finally letting go of Eileen's hand and laying it to rest on the blanket. I didn't have the heart to say out loud what I already knew to be true: Not even Lady Ophelia's expertise could help Eileen now.

Gateau jumped into my lap, and I picked her up so that I could move back and let Ophelia do her job.

The doctor soon shook her head, her long, blond hair swishing from side to side. She looked up at me sadly. "I'm afraid she's gone." She ran a manicured hand over Eileen's soft white hair, smoothing a few strands away from her forehead, and then tucked the woolen blanket I'd found up under Eileen's chin.

Benedict looked as sad as I felt. "Oh, poor Eileen. I've known her most of my life. She was a lovely woman, so kind and warm. Never had a bad word to say about anybody." He looked at Ophelia. "What did she die of?"

"It will take a postmortem to be certain. I don't know her medical history, obviously."

"She had angina," I told them. "She was on medication. She had a bad spell yesterday when we had tea together." I asked Ophelia, "Is it possible her medication wasn't working?"

She nodded. "Yes, sometimes the dosage level needs changing. That would be something her doctor would monitor. I would need to take a look at her prescription to say anything for certain. I assume she would have her pills in her bag."

I went to the till and rooted around for her handbag. It was brown with a shiny gold clasp, which opened with a snap. Inside was a tube of lipstick, a pocket mirror, a packet of tissues, keys, and a white blister pack of pills. I held them up. "Is this it?"

"Yes," she said, taking them from my outstretched hand. She turned the packet over. "And we have to call the emergency services for an ambulance. And also to alert the police. Since we don't know the exact cause of death, there will have to be a postmortem and an inquest."

"But she was old and had heart trouble," Benedict said.

"Even if it's more likely than not that her death was from natural causes, at this stage, we can't say for sure." She looked at the two of us, both so shaken by a death, and said, "I'll make the call." And she stepped outside.

Benedict stepped closer to me. "Was she—were you able to..."

"I was with her when she passed."

"Good. I wouldn't like her to have died alone."

I let out a deep sigh and shook my head slowly from side to side, as if I'd been swimming underwater and was trying to release trapped water. I was in shock. Deep shock. It was hard to believe that Eileen had passed away in front of me.

"Ambulance is on its way," Ophelia said as she came back inside. She also had the presence of mind to turn the open sign to closed.

She laid a hand on Benedict's forearm. "Does Eileen have any family? We will need to inform her next of kin."

"I don't know," he said. "She lives alone in a cottage, but I've never seen her with any family."

"She has a nephew," I piped up, suddenly springing back to life. "I don't know if her sister's still alive or where she might be, but there is definitely a nephew. She showed me some photographs yesterday." What was his name again? I thought hard. "I think his name is Timothy."

I cast my mind back. And then my thoughts began to race as I played and replayed the events of the previous day over in my head. I honed my mind's eye in on the photographs of the nephew, which were proudly displayed on the mantelpiece above the fireplace. One as a young boy and then as a married man. I recalled how Eileen had told me that she didn't see him so often anymore, and the strange expression that had accompanied that statement—sorrowful, yes, but also a little strained. I got the impression that maybe their relationship was a tricky one.

And that's when it hit me, just like the man himself almost did: the reckless driver of the silver car who'd nearly run me over and who looked strangely familiar to me. It was the man from Eileen's photos. Her nephew had almost killed me.

No wonder I couldn't place him in the moment––I'd never actually met the man, but I was certain he was the man in the car. But why on earth was Timothy driving through Broomewode today? Was it possible that he'd just been visiting Eileen? Was he the last person to speak to her before me? Had he upset her? Or even, dare I think it, triggered a heart attack?

A shiver went down my spine. It was too dreadful to even contemplate.

I must have been silent for a while because as Benedict stepped out to wait for and direct emergency services, Ophelia gestured for me to sit next to her on one of the stools by the till and said, "You must be in shock, Poppy. It's an awful thing to see a person pass away. I'll never forget the first time it happened to me when I was a young medical student. Even today, as a doctor with many years' experience, it still gets to me. It's not something you get used to."

How could I tell Ophelia that this was *not* the first time I'd set my eyes on a dead body without sounding like I had a penchant for disaster? I decided that she probably didn't need to know the ins and outs of Poppy's World right now. But she was *so* right: seeing a dead body wasn't something you got used to. She should try seeing the post-dead. I looked down at Eileen, who seemed to be peacefully asleep. If only that was the case. Her spirit had passed on, though. I didn't think I'd be visited by her. Not like I was with Gerry.

I tried to speak and cleared my throat. "Is there anything I could have done?" I struggled to get the words out. "You know, to help her?"

"Oh, Poppy," Ophelia said, her long sheet of blond hair falling forward as she reached out to clasp my hands. She was wearing a cream linen jumpsuit that was so simple and elegant, it looked as if it had been made to her exact measurements. "Eileen was an elderly lady with a heart condition. You got her medical aid as fast as you could. There's nothing else you could have done. It was her time."

I was grateful for the comfort she offered me. Not only was she super-smart, brave, and gorgeous—she was *kind*. I hoped that Benedict knew how good he had it. If Eve's insight into the local gossip was right, and Benedict had shied away from making a more serious commitment to Lady Ophelia, then he was an even stranger guy than I already thought. He needed to propose to this woman, like yesterday.

"What's happened here?" Jonathon was in the doorway of the shop. There was a smear of white flour on his black denim shirt and on the side of his cheek. Anyone would think *he'd* been the one baking today, not putting us contestants through our paces.

I pulled away from Ophelia as Jonathon walked in and looked with astonishment at the body on the floor.

"Is that Eileen?" he asked, his blue eyes wide and full of alarm.

Ophelia jumped up and stepped in front of the dead woman. "I put the closed sign on the door."

Jonathon tore his gaze away from Eileen. "I didn't see a

closed sign. I saw the woman lying on the ground. You should have locked the door to keep people out." And he stepped back and did it himself. But he stayed on our side of the locked door.

Before Ophelia tried to throw him out, I said, "I think she suffered a heart attack. I knew she was suffering from angina. She said she wasn't feeling well. I was going to drive her home. Then all of a sudden, she...collapsed. And then she was gone."

Jonathon looked genuinely sad. "Poor Eileen. That's terrible. She's been here ever since the show started filming. Elspeth's known her for years. And even though this was my first season, she made me very welcome when we came in to do the book signing for the shop. Like we were her own family."

I nodded. "That's exactly how she made me feel, too."

Jonathon turned to me. "Come on, Poppy, let's get you back to the inn. There's nothing else you can do here now." He looked across the room and smiled a small smile, far from his usual boyish grin. "And Gateau, too."

I'd almost forgotten about my sweet kitten. I picked her up, and she nuzzled herself into the crook of my arm. I stroked her soft head and immediately felt soothed.

"I can't leave," I began, but Ophelia agreed with Jonathon. "You two will only be in the way when the ambulance gets here." She promised that if the police had any questions for me, she would send them to the inn.

The three of us walked out of the gift shop and turned up the path toward the inn. I was still stunned by what had just happened, and I didn't know what to say. Clearly neither did Jonathon. But just having him by my side helped. My mind began to slow down its manic whirring, and that's when I remembered what Eileen had said to me just as she was drawing her last breath.

At the time, I was too disturbed to take it in properly, but now the words flooded back in all their strangeness: "The letter... Key is the frog. Must... I'm so sorry."

What could it all mean?

he sun had disappeared behind the clouds. No birds were singing, and the air itself was still, almost static. I couldn't help but feel that it, too, was in mourning for Eileen.

Even on a dismal afternoon, if anything could sooth me, it was nature. Usually baking would have the same effect. I could forget about anything if I got busy making marzipan or gently melting chunks of dark chocolate in a bain-marie. But now, even just the thought of having to make a showstopper cake tomorrow was more than I could bear.

I couldn't banish Eileen's last words from my head. They buzzed in my busy mind, niggling away without letting up. Letter. Frog. Keys. Must. So sorry. I let myself linger on these words, arranging them and then rearranging them. Must. Frog. So sorry. Keys. Letter. What had she meant?

I hoped Gerry was back in my room. Even though he could be annoying, Gerry's new spirit status meant that he was an excellent listener, and it wasn't exactly like he had loads of other stuff to do. Maybe he could help me crack the code.

"Poppy? Did you catch what I just said?"

I snapped out of my reverie to find that Elspeth had joined Jonathon and I at the entrance to the pub. I hadn't even noticed us walking through the door; I guess I'd been on autopilot. But now, here was Elspeth's familiar face before me: kind gray eyes, elegant nose, high cheekbones so perfectly powdered. Unlike Jonathon, with his mucky shirt, she looked every bit as pristine as she had hours earlier. But instead of her usual calm expression, worry was etched across her forehead.

"I said that I've just heard about Eileen Poole. I was on my way back to the inn when I saw the ambulance and that lovely Benedict Champney. He told me what happened. It's awfully sad. I'm so sorry you had to witness that, Poppy. It hasn't been your day, has it?"

I put Gateau down, and she scampered back outdoors. I guess she needed some cat time.

The three of us walked into the pub, and Jonathon went to the bar to order three coffees. I asked for mine to be black and as strong as Eve could make it, and resisted asking for it also to be dosed with a slug of bourbon. Even if we all were part of the same coven, Jonathon and Elspeth still felt a bit like my witchy parents.

At five p.m., the pub was quiet. The staff was preparing for the Saturday-night dinner rush, setting up tables with cutlery and glasses, placing reserved signs, a time and a name written across their black slate surface in white chalk. I caught Eve's eye at the bar. She raised her brows in concern. Jonathon must be midway through explaining what had happened to Eileen. I mouthed back that I was okay. She nodded, giving me a look to say, "We'll talk later."

Jonathon came back with the coffees—a frothy cappuccino for Elspeth, a latte for himself. I blew across the top of my cup and then took a sip of the steaming liquid. Eileen's last words entered my thoughts again. Keys. Frog. Letter. What "must" happen? And why was she "so sorry"? I thought for a moment before deciding that Elspeth and Jonathon might be able to help me solve my puzzle. If I couldn't confide in two older members of the coven, then who *could* I trust? I wasn't going to be able to work out what Eileen's last words had meant without a little backup.

So I took a deep breath and repeated what Eileen had said to me to Jonathon and Elspeth.

"What on earth could it mean?" Elspeth asked. "It certainly sounds like she wanted to tell you something important."

"I know," I said, sighing. "That's why I'm so worried. What if I can't make heads or tails of it? I couldn't live with myself knowing that I'd let someone's last words disappear into the air like a puff of smoke. I feel a great responsibility to Eileen."

Jonathon rubbed his temples, a habit I'd noticed him doing when he was trying to memorize his recipe tips. "Well, the letter bit is the most straightforward part. Did she want to send one? Maybe there's a letter ready to go that she wants posted?"

Elspeth nodded. "Or one destroyed." She smiled. "After I go, there are a few things I wouldn't want found." I imagined, her being a celebrity, she'd want to be extra careful about her legacy.

There was also that letter from Canada I'd found on the

kitchen table. A letter from an old friend didn't seem like much, but Eileen had pushed it under the cookbooks, presumably so I wouldn't read its contents. If it was a love letter from a man in his eighties, would she really care if it was found? I supposed she'd given me tacit permission to read the letter. Or try and work out what letter she was referring to.

I immediately told Elspeth and Jonathon about the letter and its Canadian address. And since I was blurting it all out anyway, I also told them that I was ninety-nine percent positive that her nephew had almost run me over today. I relayed the whole story: my jog back to the inn during the last break, the swerving silver car, how I'd stopped the car by magic—at least I thought I had. That or Eileen's nephew had excellent reflexes and even better brakes.

At that last detail, Elspeth's eyebrows shot up. In a whisper, she said, "Goodness, Poppy. I'm so glad I gave you that protection spell. But are you sure you're saying it right? So many mishaps seem to be coming your way."

I assured her I was reciting my spell, but there was no accounting for other people's reckless behavior, especially when they were behind the wheel of a car. I'd seen some terrible road rage in my time, even in the quiet lanes of Somerset.

"But really, my safety right now is beside the point," I said, shrugging. "I distinctly remember Eileen telling me that she didn't see her nephew and his wife very much anymore. Could it have been only a coincidence that he turned up in Broomewode the very next day? And he was certainly in a foul mood. He was driving like a maniac, and he didn't even stop to apologize. Just glared right at me like it was *my* fault, then shot off."

Jonathon shook his head. His usually lively eyes were flat and clouded over with sorrow. "I don't know about you, but I comfort-eat in times of crisis."

Yes, a man after my own heart. I'd been feeling peckish since we left the gift shop.

"I've got a box of chocolates in my room upstairs," he continued. "I was sent them from the boutique chocolatier hoping for an endorsement. We can share them while we brainstorm this riddle."

He looked at Elspeth. She raised an eyebrow but gave a small nod. It was almost like Jonathon was asking for her permission.

"He really does have the sweetest tooth of anyone I've ever met," Elspeth said.

"I guess that's why he went into baking," I replied.

With Jonathon gone, I decided now was a good time to share what I'd learned at Eileen's house about Valerie. I quickly explained what I'd learned about the garden parties and the staff at Broomewode Hall, then pulled out the photograph that was still in my pocket. I pointed at the woman who might be my mom.

"This is her," I said quietly, almost holding my breath as I waited to see what Elspeth would say.

Elspeth leaned over the photograph. I could smell her green, figgy perfume. A great warmth spread through my body. "The mouth," she whispered. "You have the same mouth."

It was such a relief to share my findings. "That's exactly what I thought, too. And the timing adds up. Eileen wrote the date on the back of the photo." I gestured for her to turn it over. "It's possible she could already be pregnant with me in that photo. Seeing this makes me feel so close to finding out about my origins. Until now, I kept coming up against brick walls each time I made a new turn. But this feels like proof. The resemblance is so clear."

Elspeth smiled. "Remember what I said when I first told you that you were a water witch? I could see that you were trying to understand the world and your own place within it. You've kept your heart and mind open, and now I think you may be coming closer to knowing where you came from."

I nodded. Elspeth had told me that since my mom was a witch, if I was patient, then someone from the coven would eventually remember who she was. But my biggest clue since first being mistaken for Valerie had come from Eileen, who wasn't even a witch. I was about to share my musing about this, but then Jonathon returned, brandishing a very pricey-looking box of chocolates.

I guessed my excitement about the photograph could go on hold for now. I'd already let Eve and Elspeth in on my secret. For now, Jonathon would have to remain on the outside. I decided to talk with Elspeth further once we'd figured out the mystery of Eileen's last words.

Jonathon took a seat and offered the candy around. I took a square that turned out to be chocolate-covered salted caramel and let the flavor melt in my mouth.

"I was thinking," Jonathon said, reclining slightly and taking a second truffle, "that even if the nephew is in town, it doesn't explain what else Eileen was trying to tell you. What about the set of keys? And the frog? Do you think she was trying to tell you about a hiding place? Maybe she was telling you how to let yourself into the cottage?"

Elspeth was about to say something when Penelope rushed into the pub. We stopped our conversation and turned to watch her. Penelope's face was red, her eyes puffy from crying, and I noticed that her cardigan had been wrongly buttoned and it hung askew from her slender shoulders. Poor Penelope. She'd just lost her oldest friend. She went straight to the bar where Eve was pouring a pint of ale.

"Oh, Penny," Eve said. "I'm so sorry. I just heard. Eileen was such a lovely woman. She's going to be missed around here." Eve reached out and clasped Penelope's hand.

Penelope let out a sob. "She was my best friend. We've seen each other almost every day for seventy years. Now she's gone. What will I do without her?"

Penelope was distraught, and her voice carried over to our table.

"I just called her nephew," Penelope continued, "to tell him, and he didn't even sound upset. Just quiet. That boy is so cold." She sighed. "He's in London, of course, but said he could be down here for tomorrow to help with the arrangements."

Elspeth and Jonathon looked at me at the same time with matching expressions of bewilderment. I shared their confusion. I was certain that the driver was the same man in Eileen's family photograph. Why would he lie about his whereabouts to Penelope?

Eve finished pouring her round, handed over the pints to her customer, and left the bar with two glasses of what looked to be brandy in her hands. She guided Penelope to a corner table by the window, and they sat down, no doubt to make a quiet toast to Eileen's life. Bless Eve, she really did have a heart of gold.

I leaned in closer to Elspeth and Jonathon and, in a whisper, said, "This doesn't add up. The nephew was definitely in the village today, and if he's not here now, he's certainly nearby. Why would he lie and say he was in London?"

"He could be back in London," Jonathon said. "The drive from here is about three hours, depending on traffic."

"And the way you described his driving style, Poppy, he wouldn't waste a moment."

I hadn't liked the man. He'd not stopped to see if I was all right after he'd nearly killed me, he'd lied to Penelope, and I was pretty sure he'd upset Eileen, possibly enough to cause a heart attack. And then I had a terrible thought. "If he does turn up tomorrow and visits Eileen's cottage, he might start throwing out her belongings."

"Before he's even certain the cottage will go to him?" Elspeth asked.

I relayed my worry. "Surely the first thing the nephew would do is chuck away loose bits of paper. What if the letter Eileen is talking about is really important? He might chuck it."

Elspeth looked worried, an expression that I seemed to be really good at conjuring up on people around me. Jonathon offered the box, and I chose something that had an almond on top of it. He helped himself to a square with a coffee bean perched on top. Elspeth had more willpower than either of us and refused another chocolate.

"If he's her next of kin, he'll probably inherit her house, and he looks like the sort who'd throw away all her things," I continued. "He'd probably knock the lovely old cottage down and build some kind of monstrosity in its place." I shuddered, recalling how beautiful the cottage was—not to mention its tenderly looked-after garden. "He'll probably sell it and all her memories."

I stopped. This line of thinking was upsetting, and I hated the idea that Eileen's nephew could come in and sweep away her life like it was nothing. And I was also trying to butt out the dreadful thought that kept reentering my mind: What if he even had something to do with her death? Yes, Eileen had a heart condition. I'd seen firsthand how that had affected her. She'd displayed all the usual symptoms I'd witnessed with my own eyes when we'd had tea. But she was also on medication that appeared to neutralize her discomfort immediately. And she had an active life, full of friends. Despite her wobble yesterday, there was nothing about Eileen that indicated to me that she was on the brink of a heart attack. I'd have to find a way to ask Lady Ophelia if Eileen was indeed on the right medication.

"Poppy, you must be careful," Elspeth said. "It's no good to be jumping to conclusions. I can see that your mind is working double-time, but you're on dangerous ground here."

As Elspeth spoke, the anonymous note I'd received last week came rushing back to me. *You are in terrible danger. You shouldn't be here.*

Was I being a total fool right now? Danger *was* coming at me from all angles. But no way was I going to leave the show. I'd have to find a way to stay safe but also do the right thing. And I knew that meant getting to the bottom of Eileen's last words.

As if she could read my mind, Elspeth said, "I think the best idea is for you to say your protection spell, have a hot, soothing bath, and then get a good night's sleep tonight. Remember, you have a big day ahead of you tomorrow. And no good decisions are made when we're emotionally frazzled. Rest, and then revisit Eileen's last words tomorrow, after the show and when you're feeling fresh and centered." She had a worried frown between her brows. "Tomorrow's the showstopper, and I don't have to tell you, dear, that you aren't in the strongest position at the moment."

I gulped. She didn't have to tell me. I'd come in fifth, twice. Out of eight remaining contestants. I was one disastrous showstopper away from baking-show annihilation.

But to my surprise, Jonathon disagreed. "I don't know, Elspeth. This is important stuff. Remember Eileen's kindness? You've been on the show far longer than me. Don't you want to make sure we do the right thing?"

Elspeth shot him the same kind of stern look I'd seen her give him when he messed up his rehearsed lines on set. I realized then that Jonathon usually followed Elspeth's lead on, well, *everything*.

And then I heard a familiar voice. "I have to say, Pops, I agree with you and Jonathon on this one."

I guess I'd brought this one on myself, wishing for my sidekick earlier. Gerry was floating a few meters from our table with a cheeky expression plastered across his face. His red hair was sticking out in wild tufts. I bet he wouldn't have chosen that bright red shirt with the cars and trucks all over it if he'd realized he'd be wearing it for eternity.

Jonathon looked at his watch. "Look, it's still early. The rest of the bakers went on a walk together to the next village. Euan had heard something about a fromagerie that still cuts cheese wheels with a wire like they used to, and everyone was very charmed. They'll be at least another hour. Poppy, why don't you and I go take a look at Eileen's home later tonight, ahead of the nephew's arrival tomorrow?"

Gerry immediately flashed me two thumbs-up. "And that's a ten out of ten plan from Jonathon," he said, grinning. "I'd love to come, but I'm still stuck between here and the tent."

Thank goodness.

I wanted to ask Gerry if he'd made any progress finding the author of my warning note yet, but since I was still in public, that particular chat would have to wait.

"I don't like it," Elspeth said.

"We'll be careful," I promised her. What was the worst that could happen?

CHAPTER 13

*T*hated to go against Elspeth's wishes––she was my witchy godmother, after all––but I was determined to do the right thing by Eileen. And since Jonathon was on board for a little sleuth time, I felt safe about our plan to head to Eileen's cottage once night fell.

Jonathon and Elspeth returned to their rooms so that when the other contestants returned from their walk, it wouldn't look like they were playing favorites. With all that was going on, I'd almost forgotten that they were the revered judges of *The Great British Baking Contest.* I was supposed to be quivering in my baking boots around them, not planning a nighttime detective mission. But I had to admit that getting to spend time with Jonathon and Elspeth was a privilege I was enjoying. Even if no one was around to witness it, I still felt a bit like the golden contestant.

Gerry sat in Jonathon's now empty seat and put his face over the empty coffee cup. "I miss coffee. And chocolate. I miss tasting good food. I miss making good food."

I felt for him, I really did, but I'd just seen someone die.

Gerry looked at me. "She's gone, isn't she? The gift shop woman?"'

Now I understood his whining. Eileen Poole had moved on and he was stuck here, between worlds. "Yes," I confirmed.

To take his mind off his unfortunate fate I asked if he'd found out anything more about the note I'd received. He said, "I looked in all the rooms. No one else had a note like yours." He looked kind of sorry for me. "Which means you're the only one someone's trying to get rid of."

Great. I took my empty coffee cup to the bar and waited for Eve to finish serving so that I could switch it for something a little stronger. Though not too strong. I was going to need my wits about me later. I settled on a glass of crisp white wine and was about to tell Eve all about what happened with Eileen when a noisy group entered the pub.

By now, I was familiar with the cadences of my fellow contestants. First, I heard Hamish's booming Scottish voice, "You know I love cheese as much as I love cake." He thought about it for a second. "Nah. More."

"Don't let the judges hear you," Florence said, her tinkling laugh carrying across the room.

I swiveled on my stool and stood as the group came clattering into the bar. Everyone was carrying a paper bag stamped with a logo of a slice of oozing brie and the words La Fromagerie in black ink.

"Ah, there she is. The great wanderer," Florence said, coming to kiss my cheeks. "How was your walk? I cannot believe you missed the cheese shop. He took us to his dairy farm. We were looking for you to take you along with us, but you weren't in your room. Again."

No. I'd been with a dying woman. They'd find out soon

enough about Eileen. I did not want to talk about it. Instead, I widened my eyes as though cheese was the most important thing on my mind. "He did? That's so cool. I would have loved to go there."

Priscilla caught Eve's attention and ordered a bottle of white wine. Euan asked for a tea, and Maggie joined him. I found myself being herded by Florence (Sly had competition) to a table in the center of the room. My catch-up with Eve would have to wait.

Priscilla joined us and poured the wine. Maggie and Euan sipped their tea and talked cheesecake. But Hamish was clearly still enthralled by their trip to the dairy farm. I took a drink of the crisp white wine as he related their visit to me. The guy who owned the fromagerie was a huge fan of the show. When they all turned up at his shop, he gave them a special tour, explaining all about the cheeses he sold and where they were produced. "Every culture around the world has its own cheese," Hamish said. "And it's all made using a similar process. He told us that there are thought to be around 3,500 varieties of cheese being produced worldwide." After the shop tour, he took them to his small dairy farm, where he specialized in making cheddar.

"You know cheddar originated from Somerset," Florence chimed in.

I rolled my eyes and laughed. Like I needed an Italian-born Londoner to tell me that. "I may have an American accent, but I *was* born in Somerset. I practically grew up on Ploughman's sandwiches made from Somerset cheddar." I'd loved it when my parents took me to the town of Cheddar. I remembered demanding to visit the towns of Cake, Candy and Gingerbeer.

Florence laughed it off. "Well, I'm telling you, this chap's cheddar was the finest I've ever tasted. It was succulent in texture, full-bodied with fruity undertones."

"Are you sure you're talking about the cheddar, Florence?" Priscilla leaned in. "The dairy farmer did happen to be quite the dish himself."

Florence tossed her hair, and the two of them clinked wineglasses—co-conspirators in flirtation. Euan shifted in his seat, looking uncomfortable. Priscilla and Euan had struck up a sweet friendship from the first week, but could he have deeper feelings developing beneath the surface? I would have pondered more on this if Hamish hadn't cut in.

"Did you know that cheese has seasons? Just like fruit and veg? It all depends on the effects the weather has on the soil and pastures that the animals then graze on. So some cheeses are better at particular times of the year."

"I had no idea," I said, impressed.

"Now, in late spring, is a really good season for cheese, as the temperature means the cows and goats are grazing on pastures full of soft flowers and herbs."

I thought about how cool it would be to visit the dairy farm and see if I could sketch the flowers and herbs there. But that would have to wait. I listened to the others chatting about their trip to the village and wished that I had joined them. I was missing out on all the off-screen fun.

But if I'd gone, Eileen could have died alone. I wouldn't have wanted that. Tonight was about dedicating myself to helping Eileen after she had so selflessly helped me.

I checked my watch. I was due to meet Jonathon in two hours, which would give me plenty of time to enjoy my present company, eat an early supper, and figure out exactly how to break into Eileen's cottage without ending up in Sgt. Lane's handcuffs. Although that wasn't such a bad thought either...

As soon as it began to get dark, a strange sensation spread throughout my body. I tried to ignore it and took the final bite of my cheeseburger and polished off the remaining three sweet potato fries. But I couldn't shake the feeling that something was calling me. All of a sudden, I felt like something was pulling me toward the door of the pub. I snapped my head up and looked at the entrance, and there was Jonathon's shadowy silhouette waiting for me. Whoa. That was a neat bit of magic. We'd agreed earlier to meet on the other side of the car park so no one would see us leave together.

I excused myself from the table, telling the gang that I had to go and feed Gateau before she left me for a more attentive cat mom, and said I'd come back down later for a nightcap.

I quickly ran up to my room with treats from my dinner and put out fresh food and water. Gateau was asleep on my bed, and not even my clattering about woke her as I changed into dark denim jeans and a black wool jumper. I pulled my hair up into a high ponytail, then slipped my Converse sneakers back on. They were white, which wasn't ideal for sneaking into someone's house, but they were all that I had. Maybe Jonathon could cast some kind of blanketing spell on us.

Outside, I found Jonathon waiting at the end of the narrow pebbled path that led away from the inn and the manor house to the car park. The puffy leaves of the white-beam trees that flanked us swayed gently in the breeze, and I was glad of my sweater. Jonathon was still wearing a black jacket over jeans and a baseball cap was pulled down low over his eyes.

"Take a car or walk?" he asked me when I reached him.

"The car will be quicker, but what if someone saw us driving together?" That would not look good. If we walked, I thought we could be more inconspicuous.

Jonathon agreed and asked me to lead the way. I prattled on about my cheeseburger as we walked. I was super nervous. I'd never really spent any time alone with Jonathon, and although he was also a witch, he didn't have the same calming effect on me that Elspeth had. Instead, I was overly conscious that Jonathon was a judge on the show, the harsher of the two, and I still felt a need to impress him somehow. Like I should be walking along while flipping the perfect pancake or something.

But Jonathon seemed to be at ease, maybe even excited at the prospect of doing some detective work. He told me that he wished his powers were advanced enough to cast a spell of invisibility, but instead he'd spent the last hour practicing one that would get us inside Eileen's cottage without breaking anything. I listened as he talked, taking in how eerie it felt to retrace my steps to Eileen's at night. The village was so quiet with the shops closed, and everyone seemed to be tucked into their homes. The only noise came from a small pub by the village green. I could smell the purple hyacinths that grew in neat rows by the green.

Before long, we reached the residential street where Eileen's cottage stood. I pointed it out to Jonathon.

"What a charming place," he said.

"Tell me about it. I had major cottage envy when I first saw it. You should see it bathed in golden sunlight."

I took a good look up and down the street, but it was deserted. We walked toward the cottage, and a weird chill went down my spine. But I didn't have time to linger on why that might be. We had to make sure there weren't any passersby on the street or twitching curtains to be witness to our little exploit. Not that it was really necessary; Eileen's cottage was so secluded. But still, better safe than sorry. I didn't want any nosy neighbors messing with our plan. Although come to think of it, what exactly was the plan for getting inside?

"About that spell," I said to Jonathon. "Now would be a good time to use it?"

"Right." Jonathon strode down the path to the door. He cleared his throat. "So, it went something like this: *I call on the powers who have the key / that there may be a way inside this place for me / by the shifts of the moon...*"

He stopped and turned to me. "Hold on, I'll remember the next bit a second."

I sighed. Get it together, Jonathon. No wonder he had to memorize his cookbook lines.

He began again, but then I saw something that made my heart soar. Next to the terracotta pots filled with primroses was a stone frog.

"Jonathon," I whispered. He carried on muttering something about needing a chicory plant. "Jonathon," I repeated with more urgency. "Look."

He stopped and followed to where I was pointing.

"Key... Frog," he said, repeating some of Eileen's last

words. "I must have misheard her. I bet she was trying to say, "Key under the frog."

I bent down and lifted the stone frog. Sure enough, a single silver key in a clear plastic bag was on the ground.

Bingo.

Jonathon looked relieved. "No need for magic, after all. Eileen wanted you to go inside the cottage."

As soon as he said it, I felt it to be true. Eileen wanted me to find a letter. I hoped it would be self-explanatory which one she meant when I got inside. Something already addressed and stamped that said "Urgent" on it would be good. I slipped the key into the door, and it opened easily.

Jonathon followed me, and in the darkness, I entered the hallway and headed straight for the kitchen. "The letter I saw yesterday was on the oak table," I told him, pushing open the kitchen door. "And Eileen pushed it under a stack of cookbooks."

"Do you think that's the letter she meant?"

"I don't know." I wished Eileen had had more time to be explicit about what she wanted me to do.

"That looks like a stack of books, there," he said.

"Dare we flip on a light?"

"Let's try and manage with moonlight and night vision." Jonathon picked up the stack of books, but there was no letter.

"She must have thrown it away," he said. "Perhaps she meant another letter. Is there an office?"

The moonlight was streaming in through the kitchen window. I cast my eyes around the room, frantically scanning the countertops to see if the letter had been moved. I checked on top of the microwave (where I stash my coupons and take-out menus and the odd bill I want to avoid) but still nothing.

Meanwhile, Jonathon had left the kitchen and soon called me. I found him upstairs in a small room that contained a single bed with a handmade quilt on it in red, white and blue, a small dresser and an antique desk.

This room overlooked nothing but the back garden and the fields behind it. I closed the old wooden shutters and turned on a bedside lamp. Surely no one would see the light. Jonathon pulled down the first drawer, and in unison, our jaws dropped to the ground.

"Oh no, it looks like Eileen kept every letter she's ever received," I wailed. Neatly filed were stacks and stacks of letters.

Jonathon opened the other drawers, each one filled with paper. I groaned, but he picked up a handful and passed it to me, then took another for himself. "Let's get stuck in."

With no other candidate, I was becoming certain that she wanted me to find that letter I'd seen on her table yesterday. I told Jonathon to keep his eyes open for it. "The address was from Oliver Jones in Vancouver, Canada."

"Handwritten?"

"Yup, and it was written in flowing blue ink, like from a fountain pen, in a sloping script. But couldn't you cast a sorting spell? It would make life a lot easier."

Jonathon shook his head and frowned a little. "Elspeth is much better at that sort of thing than I am. I have trouble remembering spells."

What was the use of magic if you couldn't remember spells?

I took my stack of letters to the bed and went through

them. She'd organized everything by date and very tidily too. I was holding all her correspondence for the past six months. I didn't want to spend hours here just in case that nasty nephew of Eileen's decided to show up, so I went through them quickly. She had more letters than most people, but she wasn't completely old fashioned. There was an up-to-date computer on the desk as well. However, she hadn't asked me to delete an email. She'd said letter. To me, that meant paper and envelope.

Jonathon flipped through the letters from 2019, then opened the next drawer down, which contained all her bills, neatly collected by date. He let out a long whistle. "Impressive. I'm going to have to reorganize my own filing system when this is all over."

The letters went back to Eileen's girlhood. I groaned. It looked like she'd kept every letter she'd ever received. I flipped through stacks of them but couldn't find one with Oliver's name on it. How strange.

I looked at my watch. We'd been here for twenty minutes already, and my nerves were frazzled.

"Do you think she might have thrown out the letter?" I asked Jonathon, trying not to despair. "I so don't want to go through the trash."

He threw up his hands. "Okay, okay, I'll take a glance in the bins. But you owe me." I replaced the letters where I'd found them. If there was something Eileen had wanted me to find, I hadn't come across it. The only thing that seemed significant was that she, who had kept every letter she ever received, hadn't kept the one from an old friend.

I turned out the light and followed Jonathon back to the kitchen. But while poor Jonathon had his head in the trash, I recalled the tea we'd had together. The budgies began to tweet, and I wondered who would take care of them? Penny, maybe. I didn't know much about caring for birds, but when I went into the front room, I could see there was water and seed in the cage and the door was wide open, though the two of them sat on perches looking forlorn. As though they knew.

I wondered if Eileen had had an inkling that her time was limited. I remembered seeing a doctor's appointment on her calendar. And, now I really thought about it, she'd also had a lawyer's appointment booked.

I returned to the kitchen. The Van Gogh calendar wasn't on the wall where I'd seen it only yesterday. In its place was a framed photograph of irises.

What could that mean?

"Poppy, there wasn't anything in the garbage, but look what I found in the drawer with the cutlery?" Jonathon was waving a piece of paper. "Her will," he said with a flourish.

"Oh, we shouldn't read that."

"Too late," Jonathon said. "I took a quick glance, and guess what: She's left everything to a Timothy Balentine."

"That must be the nasty nephew," I said, shaking my head. "Eileen was so organized. Why would her will be in the cutlery drawer?" I did another quick search of the kitchen. "Was there a calendar in the garbage?"

"No. Who throws away a calendar in May?"

I looked again at the irises on the wall where Eileen's calendar had been hanging. I was certain she'd had an appointment with a lawyer for the following week. What if she planned to change her will and the nephew found out?

$\mathcal{I}$ arrived back at the pub with a heavy heart. I mean way down in my boots kind of heavy. I'd gone to Eileen's cottage to find some answers, but all I'd come away with was a big bunch of new questions. Where was the letter from yesterday? Why had the calendar from the wall disappeared? If Eileen hadn't thrown them away, the only reasonable conclusion was that someone had been there before us, and I had a hunch that it was that awful Timothy. I shuddered as I recalled his glaring face, furious that I'd gotten in the path of his dangerous driving. Wherever he was headed, he was in a heck of a hurry. And in light of my trip to Eileen's, his haste made him look like he was up to something devious.

Jonathon and I parted ways at the pub entrance. His blue eyes sparkled as he thanked me for being a good partner in almost-crime. I had to laugh. The one good thing that had come out of all this horrible business was getting to spend time with Jonathon. Maybe he wasn't as tough going as I'd thought.

I desperately wanted to avoid seeing the rest of the bakers and get back to my room for some serious thinking. But I also didn't want to draw attention to myself. I'd already missed out on the walk to the next village and a lovely visit to a dairy farm. I sure didn't want my fellow bakers to think that I was avoiding them. Besides, I needed friends around me, and since Gina was out on a date tonight, I had to put my sociable face on.

Inside, the pub was buzzing with Saturday-night revelers. The tapered red candles on each table had been lit, and church candles were flickering along the windowsills and in the fireplace. The scent of roasting meat drifted up my nostrils, and although I'd already eaten, I figured a dessert would go down nicely about now.

The group was where I'd left them, though I could see that Maggie had already called it a night. I waved, then went to the bar to order a slice of tonight's dessert special, strawberry pavlova and something that would calm my nerves. I figured a vodka tonic would do the job. Eve gave me a quizzical look but was too busy to ask any questions. This time I was grateful; I wasn't ready to rehash the events of the day. It all still felt too surreal. And sad.

I went to take a seat with the others, who were crowded round Amara. I hadn't spent much time with Amara on the show. I knew that she'd grown up in Jodhpur in India and was a doctor with teenage twins, one boy, one girl, who were both studying to be doctors like her. And I really liked her seasonal cake last week: strawberry and pink peppercorn, plus, come to think of it, she'd won the madeleine round, too. It would be nice to get to know her a little better tonight.

Florence shuffled down the long bench to make room for

me. I saw why the others were crowded around Amara. She was showing off a set of hand-forged fireplace tongs and explaining that she'd bought them on sale at the gift shop during our lunch break. They were beautiful, so carefully crafted. But I couldn't look at them without thinking of Eileen. This must have been one of her last sales. I shivered.

"It was half price. Can you believe it?" Amara said, raising an eyebrow.

Hamish asked her to pass it along the table so that he could take a better look.

He whistled through his teeth. "Ooh, this is a lovely piece of craftsmanship."

I couldn't stand to look at the tool. It flooded me with too many bad memories. Instead, I turned my attention to who else was dining in the pub.

In the short time I'd been at Broomewode, I'd come to think of myself as—if not exactly part of the village—then at least close to those who were. Eve and Susan Bentley were my new coven sisters, Eileen and Katie Donegal had both helped me take another few steps toward discovering my family heritage, and I was just as fascinated by the gossip about the Champney family as any of the locals.

I watched the pub patrons enjoying their Saturday night, laughing and drinking and tucking into delicious food, and for the first time allowed myself to wonder how it might feel if I *was* truly one of them: a Broomewode villager. Back in the place where my mom met my dad. Back in the place where it all began.

I soon spied Ophelia and Benedict, sharing a bottle of red in the corner. They made a very cozy scene, seemingly unperturbed by what had happened in the gift shop just a few hours earlier. I guessed that Ophelia was used to being in difficult situations and the passing of an older woman with a heart condition probably didn't count as tragedy by her war-zone standards. But still, I wondered if they, like me, were carrying the same heavy weight in their chests. Putting on a brave face.

There was something about Eileen's death that was so sudden, it chilled me to the core, and after the disappearance of Oliver Jones's letter, not to mention the strange vanishing of Eileen's calendar, I couldn't shake the feeling that something was awry. I told myself not to be paranoid, but this time my bossy inner voice would not shut up.

At least there'd be a postmortem. I imagined that meant someone would ask questions, maybe get to the root cause of how she'd died.

I was trying to muster up the courage to go and interrupt the couple's little tête a tête and ask Lady Ophelia's opinion about Eileen's medication when someone tapped my shoulder.

"Hello, again." It was Broomewode Hall's new gardener, Edward. He had a half-drunk pint of lager in his hand, and his pale skin was flushed pink. In place of his gardener's uniform, he was wearing a white shirt and blue denim jeans.

"Hi," I said, a little bemused why he'd come to say hello. We were practically strangers.

"You here for supper?" he asked, running a hand through his blond hair.

"Um, yes. Earlier. I'm waiting on a pudding, actually." He must think I was the worst chowhound, baking treats all day and then ordering more at night. "Can't seem to get enough of the sweet stuff."

Before he could reply, Florence cleared her throat—*very loudly.*

I took the hint and introduced Edward to the group, explaining that he was the new gardener for the grounds.

"Sit, sit," Florence insisted, shuffling away from me. She patted the bench, gesturing at the empty space. "Please talk about something that doesn't involve the words flour, sugar, or butter. That's the only rule for being part of our gang. Are you game?"

I cringed but had to hand it to Florence—she certainly knew how to make people feel welcome.

"I can do that," Edward said, putting his pint down and swinging a leg over the bench to slip in between us. "If you lot don't talk about grass, hedges, or string trimmers." I could tell right away he was going to fit in. "I've only just moved here from Devon, and the gardening team are a nice bunch, but they've all known each other for years. It can be intimidating."

"Oh yes, I know exactly what you mean," Florence said, flicking her reddish hair so that it fell in soft waves over her shoulders. I noticed that she'd changed the color of her polish since yesterday, and now her nails were a deep eggplant. They shone each time she waved her hands through the air.

Hamish passed Amara's tongs along the table. Just like Hamish, Edward whistled through his teeth to signal his appreciation. What was it with men and tools?

"Now that's a beauty," he said. "The base metal has been shaped on an anvil using hot coals and a hammer." He turned the object over in his hands, which were large and sturdy. At some point, he'd damaged one of his fingernails so

it had a thick crack in it. "See that nice texture and matte rich-
ness to the finish? That's done with beeswax."

At the mention of beeswax, my ears pricked up. Maybe
Susan had been supplying Reginald with wax from her bees,
and that's why they were so close?

"You sound like you know what you're talking about,"
Priscilla said, giving Edward a toothy grin.

"My granddad was a blacksmith in Devon. He never quite
got over how my dad didn't want to continue the family trade,
so granddad used to chew my ear off about blacksmithing
when I was a boy. He taught me the trade, sure, but my heart
was always in the outdoors. Need that fresh air and nothing
but the sky over my head. My uncle took over the business in
the end, so granddad's legacy continues."

I told Edward and the rest of the group that I'd met Reginald McMahan, the local blacksmith who made the tools
right here in Broomewode. "He's self-taught, actually. He only
began blacksmithing after he retired."

But Edward scoffed at my comment and said, "Is this from
the gift shop?"

Amara nodded. "Yes, why?"

"Whoever did this has been at his trade for years and
years. Decades, probably. This isn't amateur stuff. I told the
lady who runs the gift shop the very same thing when I first
got here."

I felt my mouth drop open. There was something innately
trustworthy about Edward. But if what he was saying was
true, then how had Reginald become so good? The story
around the village was that he'd been something in finance in
"the city," which in the UK pretty much always meant
London. Then he'd retired to Broomewode and taken up

blacksmithing. Was he lying? And which was he lying about? The career in finance? Had he been forging fireplace tools for all the years he'd pretended to be a financier? Because how could he fake being a good blacksmith?

"Anyone who claims he picked up this trade in a few wet weekends is having you on," Edward said, handing the tongs back to Amara. "But whoever it was that made these, well, they're a fine craftsman. How much did you pay?"

She told him.

"You got a bargain, for sure," he said to her, nodding, which made her puff up with delight.

"It's for my husband for his birthday. He will be so happy."

I didn't know what to make of Edward's judgment. Was it possible that Reginald was a blacksmithing prodigy? Or was he really pulling the wool over our eyes—especially poor Susan's. For her sake, I hoped not. But I couldn't let this go without finding out more from Susan herself. I vowed to find time to speak with her after the showstopper challenge. Wow, my to-do list was growing bigger by the hour.

But first, I wanted to catch Ophelia and Benedict before they slipped away for a romantic moonlight stroll or whatever it was that aristocratic couples did for fun in the countryside on Saturday nights.

Luckily, all the women at the table were fussing over Edward, and Hamish, Euan and Daniel were discussing the latest football results. So after a big gulp of my vodka tonic, I slipped away and headed for the couple's cozy table.

Benedict looked up as I approached. He looked smart in a dark-colored shirt that looked both expensive and recently ironed, but his eyes were troubled. "Hello, Poppy," he said, in a tone that wasn't quite welcoming. When I saw him in his proper element, dressed like a tall, dark and handsome modern-day hottie rather than a farmhand or an antique oil painting, he had a certain appeal. I was beginning to see what Ophelia seemed so set on.

"How are you, darling?" Lady Ophelia asked, letting her hand slip from Benedict's grasp. Despite the events of the afternoon, she looked as elegant as ever. Her hair hung in a lovely golden sheet about her shoulders, and her cheeks were flushed with healthy color. I was sure that I looked like a scrappy teenager in comparison in my black sweater, jeans, and high ponytail. I shuffled uncomfortably on the spot. Now that I'd interrupted them, I wasn't sure I could bring up a dead person's medication. Not when they were obviously spending a cozy Saturday night date night together.

"Have you managed to eat something?" Ophelia asked, once more showing her genuine kindness.

I told them both I was fine, fed and watered and that I was deeply grateful for their help in the shop earlier today.

Ophelia gave me a wide smile, showing me her straight set of pearly teeth. "I'm just happy we were close by."

"I was wondering if the police said anything to you when they arrived."

"Just the usual," Lady Ophelia answered. "We explained that you'd been on the scene when Eileen passed and showed them her medication. The ambulance arrived, and then we left the paramedics to it. Don't worry, Poppy. This was all just routine."

But was it?

Benedict shifted in his chair. Clearly I was intruding, but I had to say what was whirring around in my mind, refusing to go away. I swallowed and then took a deep breath. "I just have this gut feeling. Something about Eileen's death isn't adding up." I paused, aware that I might sound crazy. But hey, what was new? I had to trust my gut. I touched my amethyst necklace for support, then directed my next comment at Ophelia, feeling Benedict's disapproval bubbling away under the surface, threatening to come out. "Do you think there could have been foul play involved?"

She leaned back as though I'd put something very pungent and smelly under her nose, but it was Benedict who replied. "I think you're letting your imagination run away from you, Poppy." His voice was stern. "Eileen was over eighty years old. She had a heart condition. As sad as it is, those two things go hand in hand with a natural death."

But after a moment of awkward silence, when I pretty much wished the floor would open up and swallow me whole, Ophelia said, looking at Benedict with an expression I couldn't quite read, "We're taught to trust our gut when we're in the field. Poppy, is there some reason you're concerned about Eileen's passing?"

I nodded, grateful that she understood.

"If you're in any doubt at all, there should be an autopsy. And the police should be informed. You need to tell them everything you know or suspect."

I swallowed. How would DI Hembly and Sgt. Lane respond to the news that Poppy Wilkinson had another mysterious death for them to investigate? I could only hope they'd be as understanding as Lady Ophelia, who was fast becoming my favorite person in all of Broomewode Village. But whatever their response, I knew I had to get to the bottom of Eileen's death, and I had to act fast—before her hot-rod nephew made things even more difficult.

"I'll put in the call," Ophelia said, ignoring Benedict's pointed glare. "Poppy, why don't you write down your number for me, and I'll let you know what they say." She produced a pen and a business card from her handbag and turned the card over on the table so that the blank side faced me.

I thanked her and scribbled down my cell number.

I hoped my instincts were right because I was opening a big can of wriggling, corpse-eating worms.

CHAPTER 15

I made my way bleary-eyed and yawning down to breakfast, my stomach already growling at the prospect of bacon and eggs on thick slices of buttery brown toast. I was wearing the second of my new shirts, and Gateau was trotting happily by my side. We'd both had a good night's sleep, despite all of my unanswered questions, probably because I'd worn myself out returning to Eileen's cottage in my mind, ransacking my memory for any detail I might have missed during our tea or last night with Jonathon. I'd come up blank each time. But that wasn't going to deter me. I'd speak with DI Hembly and Sgt. Lane as soon as the day's filming was in the can.

But when I arrived, the mood in the dining room was subdued. Instead of the usual nervous excitement, a feeling in the air that you could practically touch, everyone was quiet, heads bowed low close to their plates.

"Oh man, please don't tell me someone else has died," I whispered to Gateau. She looked at me like I'd finally lost the plot and then darted down the hallway and out into the flowerbeds by the entrance of the inn. Great. That cat really needed some lessons in witch-familiar solidarity.

Euan, Hamish and Priscilla were at one table, while Maggie and Gaurav were at another. No sign of Amara or of Florence either—but there was nothing unusual about that. She liked to make a late entrance. Maggie looked up from her bowl of fruit and yogurt and gestured for me to join them.

"What's happened?" I asked in a quiet voice, not quite wanting to know the answer.

"Filming's delayed, dear," she replied. She was wearing a beautiful lilac shirt with leaves embroidered in gold thread. The green of the leaves emphasized the hazel of her eyes. It looked so perfect you'd never know she'd been wearing it all day yesterday. I wondered if she'd washed and ironed it overnight. "Two of the ovens have short-circuited. And after what happened to poor Gerald"—she shook her head sadly —"they've closed down the tent to make repairs and to check the wiring of each oven."

"Oh no," I said, thinking about my lengthy to-do list, which I'd aimed to tackle the minute filming finished. "What about the showstopper?" Sunday was always a long day because of the showstopper, and I wanted to get going and get baking while I was fresh. I suspected we all felt the same. "Did they say how long that'll take?"

"At least two hours," Gaurav said. He was making his way through a mountain of French toast. "I don't know whether it's nice to have some extra time to get my head in gear or if it's just making me even more nervous." He smoothed down his pale gray shirt. "I'm leaning to more nervous."

"Me too, Gaurav," Maggie said, patting his arm kindly.

I'd rather be baking, but I figured this break would give

me the time I needed to do a little detective work. I glanced at the heaped buffet table. But not until I'd eaten my fill.

I asked Maggie and Gaurav if they wanted anything else, then shot straight over to the buffet table. In the silver serving dishes, a heap of hot scrambled eggs and rashers of streaky bacon were waiting for me, and I helped myself to a pretty generous portion. Two slices of toast and butter, a cup of black coffee, and then I sat back down to demolish the lot. I'd had time to wash my hair this morning too, and I was letting it air dry before Gina scooped it back up into a pony tail.

"Will you join us to watch a bit of telly?" Maggie asked when I finished, raising an amused eyebrow at the speed I ate. "They're setting up the projector to show us some rushes of last week's episode. I can't wait to see how it all looks on a big screen."

I swallowed my last mouthful of toast and shook my head. As tempting as it was, I had to make some progress toward uncovering the cause of Eileen's sudden death. I'd woken today with an even stronger conviction that something was up. I just needed to prove it. "I think I'm going to prepare for today with a nice long walk and then maybe practice my bake," I told Maggie and Gaurav. "After yesterday's performance, I really need to up my game. I'd hate to lose my spot on the show because my focus was all over the place."

Gaurav said he totally understood and would probably go back to his room to mentally practice each step of his showstopper. Maggie claimed to need the rest since she was the oldest, but I wasn't fooled. She was doing so well in the competition already that I suspected she had a real shot at winning. I guessed that she knew it, and instead of wearing herself out practicing biscuits she could make in her sleep, she'd relax for a couple of hours. I felt bad for my white lie because I really did need to practice. I just had to hope that I'd done enough in my little kitchen with Mildred by my side to get through to the next round.

I wondered if the gift shop would open today. Even though the production company tried to discourage spectators, when they showed up, they were allowed to watch so long as they stayed behind a rope set up for that purpose and kept quiet. We'd become accustomed to having an audience, but with no filming to watch, what would they do but go to the pub and the gift shop? I wondered whether they'd close today out of respect for Eileen or open out of greater respect for the bottom line. If Lord and Lady Frome had anything to do with it, I thought I could guess the answer.

Outside, it was a warm, balmy morning, as if the weather had long moved on from yesterday's tragedy. Puffy white clouds were dotted about the blue sky, but the sun's rays persevered. Birds were chirping in the trees, and I felt cheered by their song. But the feeling dissipated the moment I saw Penelope. She was wearing a black shift dress and stood gazing through the window of the gift shop, a beautiful bouquet of white flowers clasped in both hands. She bent and placed the flowers on the door of the gift shop, which was closed, the shutters pulled down. I felt mean that I'd suspected the Champneys would open the gift shop today.

I stopped in my tracks, not wanting to disturb Penelope while she honored her friend. We both stayed that way, silent and staring, Penelope lost in her thoughts and me trying to control the questions that raced through mine.

After a few minutes, Penelope wiped her eyes, and I walked to her, gently saying her name. Penelope barely knew me, but from the stories I'd heard through Eileen and the story of Oliver Jones, I felt very much connected to her.

"I met you," she said. "You're one of the bakers." She wiped her eyes with a wet hankie.

"Poppy," I said.

"That's right." She wiped her wet cheeks again, then shook her head sadly. "It doesn't feel real. Only yesterday, Eileen was bossing me about, showing me the ropes. I feel like I'm standing here waiting for her to arrive. To open the shop." She could barely finish the sentence, her voice choked by tears.

I got choked up myself listening to her, reminded of how much Eileen would be missed in this small community. How kind she'd been to me, a virtual stranger. "She made me feel so welcome," I said, telling Penelope about the tea Eileen had made me Friday. "She was helping me trace some family history, actually."

"Oh yes, that sounds like Eileen. She always made herself available to anyone who needed her. And she loved our little village." Penelope stared down at the flowers on the doorstep, smiling sadly.

I took a deep breath. "I saw a letter from your brother at Eileen's cottage. I heard he moved to Canada. When Eileen was...slipping away from us, she whispered something about a letter. She was quite distracted when we had tea, maybe even a little worried. It was the last piece of correspondence she received. Would you have any idea why Oliver might have written to Eileen?"

Obviously, I couldn't tell Penelope that I'd, in a round-about way, broken into Eileen's cottage and found that the letter had disappeared and there was no evidence of any others. I just hoped that she knew they spoke with one another and that my question wasn't entirely out of the blue.

Penelope looked into my eyes with a solemn, grave expression, almost as if she were searching for the answer to an impossible question. But then she smiled sadly. "The three of us were inseparable when we were young. You should have seen us. Always laughing and getting into mischief."

"That's the same for a lot of siblings. My best friend, Gina, has a big family, and they were like that too when we were growing up." I paused. "I don't have any siblings myself."

I do have my coven sisters, but Penelope doesn't need to know that.

"Well, Oliver had a fire in him, that was for sure. But then he started to become withdrawn. I had no idea why. We were so close, but he stopped confiding in me. He never even said goodbye when he ran away. Our poor parents were distraught. It was years before we heard from him."

Another tear slipped down Penelope's powdered face, and she dabbed at her eyes with the very wet embroidered handkerchief. The birds overhead continued to tweet and sing their sweet song, and it was so lovely, it felt cruel.

"That must have been very difficult."

Great words of comfort, Poppy. Why was it so hard to avoid pat phrases when people were grieving? I'd hoped to get better at this kind of thing. Maybe I needed to read a couple of books on the subject, learn lines the way Jonathon did.

"You know, sometimes I thought Eileen might take a trip to Canada to see Oliver, but she never did. I think she was hoping he'd come back for her. All those years she waited. And now it's too late."

I was about to ask Penelope if she knew what Oliver

might have written in his last letter to Eileen, but two very familiar figures were approaching us from the car park.

DI Hembly and Sgt. Lane both looked very smart in pressed trousers: gray for Hembly and navy blue for Lane. Each officer was wearing a white shirt, though Lane's was a softer, more relaxed fit, and he finished his ensemble with a pair of Ray-Bans. The two officers introduced themselves to Penelope, and then shook hands with me––Hembly's grip extremely brusque, Lane's still firm but far less terrifying. They both looked down at the white bouquet of flowers on the gift shop doorstep.

"I'm Eileen's best friend," Penelope told the officers. "Was," she corrected herself, her voice lowered until it was a mouse-like whisper. "Penelope Jones."

"We're so sorry for your loss," Sgt. Lane said. "This must be a very difficult time."

Okay, so at least I wasn't the only one who talked in pat phrases.

DI Hembly cleared his throat in that commanding manner of his. "Now it appears that Eileen Poole passed away from natural causes. But all unexpected deaths all have to be investigated. And after a telephone call from Lady Ophelia Wren this morning, we are pursuing the possibility that the situation may be more complicated than it first appeared." DI Hembly raised a brow ever so slightly.

I swallowed. Here I was, blindly following a hunch again. I just hoped that my witchy instinct was on point again–– otherwise this could be deeply embarrassing.

"Complicated?" Penelope said, turning pale. "I don't understand."

"There's nothing to worry about, Ms. Jones," Sgt. Lane

said. "It's normal procedure to make sure that the death was of natural causes. But we'd just like a moment with Miss Wilkinson here, as she was present at the scene."

He gave me a small smile. And then there were those dimples.

Focus, Poppy.

I felt guilty, though I couldn't pinpoint why. Something *was* fishy about Eileen's death. But how was I going to explain that to two police officers without admitting to some casual breaking and entering that really wasn't a crime because I'd found the front-door key? If I wasn't in such a tricky situation, I'd probably laugh out loud. But the expression on DI Hembly's face was enough to sober me. Sgt. Lane explained that Lady Ophelia was at the pub already and that the inn had kindly put aside a room for us to have a "little chat."

I said goodbye to Penelope, squeezing her hands tightly as I left, trying to show her how I cared. Even though I'd only known Eileen a very short while, her kindness and warm personality had made a real impression on me.

As we walked back to the inn, my mind stayed on Sgt. Lane's choice of words: "little chat." Was he humoring me? Surely they wouldn't waste police time interviewing me about Eileen's death? And wasn't Lady Ophelia Wren's support enough to demonstrate that something serious was at play here? She was a doctor, after all.

In the pub, I was disappointed to see that Eve wasn't working. A member of staff I hadn't seen before guided us into a small office, where Lady Ophelia was waiting. Her hair was pulled back in a high ponytail, and she was wearing a khaki jumpsuit, a wide cotton belt tied in a knot at her waist, and cream leather sling-backs with a kitten heel. She was sipping a latte and looked perfectly relaxed, not like she was about to be interviewed by the police at all. I guessed that this kind of thing was pretty inconsequential compared to her usual duties.

The barmaid said she'd be back with some more coffee— black for DI Hembly and me, a cappuccino for Sgt. Lane.

I took one of the office-style leather chairs next to Ophelia. The detectives faced us across the table, and I suddenly felt like I might have pushed the panic button without proper reason. But Ophelia seemed to sense this and began speaking.

"Thank you for talking with us," she said, her voice silky-smooth. "As you know, Eileen Poole passed away yesterday at the gift shop. Poppy here was with her at the time, and when she collapsed, Poppy ran to get help, and that's when I was called in. I pronounced her dead at five minutes past five."

As Sgt. Lane rapidly took notes, Ophelia continued her report of yesterday's tragic events. Our coffees arrived, and I was deeply grateful to have something to do with my hands.

"And do you agree with Lady Ophelia's account?" DI Hembly asked me. I noticed that Lady Ophelia didn't insist he drop her title. I suspected she didn't mind using it when it got her what she wanted. In this case, the full attention of the police.

I nodded. "Yes, everything she says is how it happened." I paused and stole a look at Ophelia, who gave me an encouraging smile. "But a couple of things which happened before and after Eileen's death are bothering me."

I took a deep breath and told them about my encounter with Eileen's nephew, how he'd nearly run me over, then hadn't mentioned he'd been in the village right before his aunt died.

"Did you report his dangerous driving?"

"No. I wasn't hurt. I'm more concerned that he never mentioned he'd been here only hours before his aunt died and never mentioned it."

"You were with Ms. Poole Friday as well?" Sgt. Lane asked.

"Yes. She was helping me learn about the village history. She wanted to make me scones." I left out the bit about them being awful. The detectives both looked at me blankly. "It was the scone challenge on the show yesterday," I said by way of explanation. "Anyway, after Eileen died, Penelope, her best friend, called the nephew--"

"Timothy Balentine?"

"Yes, that's right. She called him to let him know about Eileen's passing, and he said he was in London. But I'd seen him here only a few hours before Eileen died. He never said he'd been here. Why didn't he?"

DI Hembly sighed ever so slightly and leaned forward. "In times of grief or tragedy, it's very common to put two and two together and come up with five. Is it possible that the photograph and the man in the car were not actually the same but simply shared some similarities, like gray hair, for example? The mind can play tricks on us, especially if we're looking for answers."

I shook my head. *No, no, no.* I *knew* it was Timothy. But how could I prove it? I couldn't tell them about the missing letter from Oliver Jones or the calendar without admitting that I'd gone to the cottage after Eileen died.

"It's just—" I started, then stopped. "There's more. I noticed that Eileen had an appointment with a solicitor set up for next week. She asked me to fetch her angina medication when we were in the kitchen, and a calendar was hanging on the wall by the cupboard. It was set for Wednesday." There. Now if they searched her cottage they'd see that the calendar was missing.

"I'm not quite sure why that would be relevant, Miss Wilkinson." DI Hembly said it as a statement, not a question.

"I wonder if it had something to do with her will. Changing it possibly."

"That's a bit of stretch," Sgt. Lane said. "It could have been about anything."

"How many reasons would an old woman have to go to a solicitor? I know, it doesn't prove anything, but I have this feeling. I can't explain it. An instinct. Something I can't ignore."

DI Hembly gave me a look that suggested I'd be better off trying a little harder to ignore it.

But Sgt. Lane had a much softer expression. I could see that he believed me or at least believed that I was completely sure of what I'd seen.

Ophelia set her cup down. "I think there's enough doubt about Ms. Poole's death to warrant further investigation, don't you?"

I was so glad she was here. I was going to get to the bottom of all this for Eileen's sake, and now I had an aristocratic doctor backing me up, and at least half of Sgt. Lane was siding with me, too. Team Poppy was looking strong.

CHAPTER 16

*a*fter the police left, Ophelia told me that she was due back at the manor house for a video conference. She was on the board of directors for an education charity that set up schools in refugee camps across the globe. Could this woman be any nicer?

She reminded me of the earl's invitation to sketch the interiors of Broomewode Hall (as if I needed reminding!) but said that it would have to wait until tomorrow. The earl and Lady Frome were visiting friends in Bath today, and she wouldn't want to take liberties by inviting me in.

I smiled brightly at Ophelia, happy that she remembered my somewhat made-up job commission. I said I wouldn't have enough time today anyway as the showstopper was due to film in less than an hour. To calm my nerves before the competition kicked off again, I decided to sketch some of the flowers planted in the grounds of Broomewode Hall instead.

I rushed back to my room to get my sketchbook, pencils, and tote bag before meeting Ophelia outside so that we could walk through the grounds together.

But when I got upstairs, Gerry was pacing my room.

"Where have you been, Pops?" he asked, frowning.

"With the police," I said, shrugging. "Some things about Eileen Poole's death don't add up."

Gerry let out a low whistle through his teeth and then stopped abruptly. "Cooool," he said. "The whistle, I mean. I didn't know I could still do that. Shame about the gift shop lady, though. I never met her myself."

I thanked him and asked if he'd made any progress sourcing the handwriting of my warning note.

"That's what I wanted to talk to you about."

My heart began to beat faster. Had Gerry discovered who was trying to bump me off of the show?

"I know every design and recipe the other contestants are using for the showstopper."

"What are you suggesting? That I cheat in some way? I would never do that."

He looked hurt. "I'm not suggesting anything of the kind. I wanted to tell you that I think yours is the best. You could win this one, Pops." In a lower tone, he said, "And you could use the win."

"Okay, Gerry. Thank you for the vote of confidence. But I have to go. Let's chat more later."

"Poppy, Poppy, Poppy. You're the only one who I can talk to, yet you're always running off to talk to someone else. Where's the love for your old baking pal? And shouldn't you be focusing your mind on your showstopper?"

He was right, but at this point, I thought distraction might calm me down. I promised we'd catch up after the next bake. But I warned Gerry to stay away from the tent. "I'm struggling this weekend enough as it is without having to pretend I can't see the ghost in the room."

Gerry reluctantly agreed to stay away for the sake of the show. I waved goodbye, relieved, and raced down the stairs to meet Ophelia.

IT WAS A BIT SURREAL, hanging out with a distinguished and famous humanitarian. But Ophelia was fast becoming one of my favorite people. As we walked, she chatted about her latest trip to Yemen, about the kids she'd met and the doctors who worked tirelessly in the camps. When she asked me about my own work, I was almost embarrassed to talk about being a graphic designer. I mean, who could live up to her special brand of angelic endeavors? But I told her about my love of design, how I'd always been a visual person, drawn to shape and color and texture. That's what I loved about baking, too.

But with this new commission, which (I quickly added) also included flowers and plants in the grounds of manor houses, I was able to draw on my time in college, when I took modules in illustration. I loved being able to capture the natural world, especially the flowers. And there were so many to choose from in the gardens of Broomewode Hall.

Ophelia was an excellent listener, so good, in fact, that I hadn't noticed how long I'd been talking. We were already at the foot of the manor house. I suspected I'd have some time. When we'd passed the white tent there'd been a stream of red-faced people buzzing in and out, looking harassed. The electrical problem didn't look like it would be fixed anytime soon.

Ophelia had a whimsical look on her face. "Do you think I might be able to visit the set?" she asked in a half whisper. "I'm such a fan. Ben thinks it's silly and laughed when I asked him, but perhaps you might be so kind as to set up a quick visit?"

I grinned, charmed by her fan-girling. "Let me see what I can do. I'd love to say yes right away, but there are all kinds of rules and restrictions. We're not even allowed to talk about what happens during filming to anyone outside the show. Otherwise I would have dropped the gossip already. I bet everyone would be thrilled to have you visit, though."

She laughed and thanked me. I looked around the neat flowerbeds, so carefully tended by the gardeners. "Isn't it amazing?" I said, pointing to a beautiful red burst of peony. I opened my sketch book, ready to start and Ophelia looked over my shoulder. The book had opened to the sketch of foxgloves I'd made at Broomewode Farm.

"These are lovely," she said. "You're very talented."

I said. "So strange to think that they can be deadly."

"Yes, but also lifesaving," Ophelia said. "Poor Eileen's angina medication was Digoxin. It's made with digitalis, also known as foxglove. It was what kept her heart ticking."

Until it didn't.

Ophelia excused herself and said to get in touch if the police contacted me and, more importantly, to arrange a visit to the baking tent. I thanked her for everything. But as soon as she disappeared from sight, my heart began to beat out of control. A terrible thought had entered my mind as Ophelia talked about the foxglove.

I'd seen Susan drying a big bundle of foxgloves at the farm to use in some kind of tonic. But she never said what it was for. Was Susan making her own medicine? Or could it have been something more sinister?

The awful feeling continued to spread through my gut, twisting it until I was gripped with fear. Reginald's face flashed into my mind, and then Edward's comments last night.

Anyone who claims he picked up this trade in a few wet weekends is having you on.

If what Edward had said was true, and my instincts said it was, then Reginald was no blacksmith. He was an imposter. And Edward had told Eileen about his suspicions. How far might Reginald go to protect his reputation? Had Eileen confronted Reginald about his lies? Was someone else the real blacksmith?

And what did this mean for Susan? Those two obviously had a tight bond. I didn't know for sure if it was romantic, but the affection they had for one another was plain for all to see. Susan had already lost her husband—how far might a grieving widow go to protect the only other man in her life? Could she have given Eileen her own, deadly, foxglove remedy?

Despite the warm weather, I was chilled to the bone. I recalled Elspeth telling me that there were witches who used their powers of magic for good and those who chose a darker path. Maybe Susan Bentley wasn't all that she appeared to be.

CHAPTER 17

"*P*oppy? There you are! We've just been given the go-ahead to start filming."

I looked up and saw Gaurav and Hamish peering over my shoulder at my sketchbook. I blushed and closed the pages. I'd been trying to calm my racing mind by sketching a patch of woodland bluebells, and I'd lost track of time completely.

"Don't be embarrassed," Hamish said. "Those drawings are bonny. I can see why your cakes are so pretty."

I thanked Hamish, pleased with his comment. I was always worried that my illustrations weren't as good as my graphic design, so a bit of a confidence boost for this job was very welcome. Besides which, in about fifteen minutes, I was going to have to make the best showstopper of my life to save my sorry behind from being booted off the show this week.

I'd been far too distracted during the signature scones and technical brandy snaps challenge. Everything was now riding on the biscuit showstopper. And the brief was the hardest yet: to create a three-dimensional scene from our favorite children's book. Entirely made of biscuits. Showstopper? More like heart-stopper. I wouldn't be able to even dream up a more difficult challenge. But what I did know was that this afternoon's baking was really going to show up any amateur mistakes. And I couldn't afford a single slip.

Inside the tent, the usual frantic energy of cameramen, electricians, sound guys, producers, and their assistants had been heightened by the electrical failure. The director, Fiona, was pacing, and Donald Friesen, the series producer, was back on set and stressed as usual. The show couldn't afford another incident like Gerry, and although Gordon was behind bars now, the ovens remained a touchy subject. Especially for Aaron Keel, the electrician, who looked furious as he supervised a final testing of the ovens.

The rest of the contestants were already in the tent, as Hamish, Gaurav and I went to our workstations and began setting up. The uniformity of our expressions said it all: We were united by biscuit terror, dismayed by dough, cowering at the thought of chocolate chips.

Gina rushed over, brandishing a bronzer and brush. I finished arranging my ingredients and followed her to the hair and makeup chair. She'd heard all about Eileen and asked me what had happened yesterday. I wasn't in the mood to talk about the last twenty-four hours, so I promised I'd give the full rundown of my crazy Saturday the minute filming finished. Right now, I had to get my head in the game.

"I completely understand, Pops," Gina said. "I can see you're worried, but you're going to smash this challenge. I'm sure of it. You've practiced enough, and you're ready. Have faith."

I smiled. During the week, I'd driven over to Gina's at least three evenings in a row, a biscuit extravaganza carefully balanced on the passenger seat and Gateau mewing in the back, angry that her usual driving position had been replaced by a giant cookie. Gina, bless her, had helped me decide which children's book to use and then had tasted several renditions of different scenes.

After much back and forth, we'd settled on *Matilda* by Roald Dahl, which her father used to read to us both when we were kids. The winning scene depicted the moment that the dastardly Miss Trunchbull makes schoolboy Bruce Bogtrotter eat an entire cake in front of his classmates. The scene was the most complicated bake I'd ever attempted, with each child and Miss Trunchbull made from vanilla flavored biscuits, a huge triple chocolate cookie sandwich with chocolate buttercream filling to represent the cake, and an entire classroom structure made from gingerbread. Not to mention all the icing involved. There were so many variables and fiddly moments that at any moment, the whole scene could collapse.

If I could pull it off, it would be a masterpiece. But if I didn't, well, it didn't bear thinking about.

As Gina chattered away, I closed my eyes, trying to find my calm inner center.

When she showed me the mirror, I looked a lot more confident than I felt. Gina had done it again. Somehow, she knew exactly how to make my features shine. I hugged her close, and she whispered good luck in my ear.

I rushed back over to my workstation, and Florence came to say hello. Even wearing the same outfit she'd worn yesterday, Florence looked fresh and glamorous. If Florence didn't win the baking contest, surely she'd land a part in a movie.

Fiona asked for quiet, and I sidled back over to my workstation. This was it. My one chance to really shine and save myself from being sent home. This meant everything to me.

The four presenters entered the tent together, Arty linking arms with Elspeth, and Jonathon doing the same with Jilly. I could feel Elspeth's presence calm the atmosphere, and I managed to smile for the cameras, which were trained on our faces.

"All right, bakers," Jilly said. "As part of biscuit week, Elspeth and Jonathon have set a most difficult showstopper. A biscuity book. Or a bookish biscuit. You must re-create a three-dimensional scene from your favorite childhood book entirely made from biscuits."

Arty continued, "Now what kind of biscuit is entirely up to you, as is how you embellish your scene. The judges will be looking for all kinds of different shapes, textures and flavors of biscuit. You might wish to ice your biscuits, or use buttercream or perhaps some marzipan to add the detail you'll need to compete in this challenge. But however you do decide to interpret the challenge, make sure you do it with finesse and flair. This is a great opportunity to show the judges your most creative sides. Treat your dough as a potter would treat their clay. But––you must make it tasty. We're not an art gallery. I've got to want to eat it."

Even though we'd known the challenge in advance, it still felt overwhelming to hear Jilly describe it. I stole a look at the other contestants. Despite a few obligatory laughs, they all looked white with fear. Phew, I wasn't the only one.

"I know that there's a certain comedian here who loves biscuits, isn't that right?" Jilly asked in a teasing tone.

"Guilty as charged," Arty said. "I can munch my way through two packs of custard creams without stopping for air."

Everyone gave their best impressions of a laugh again.

"So I'm double excited to see what you all can manage today," Arty continued. "Will that cookie crumble? Or will our bakers rise to the challenge? Whatever happens, do not burn those biscuits! Contestants, you have four hours to pull together your showstopper. On your marks, get set... Bake!"

I gulped, but there was no time for nerves. We had four hours to pull this off, and I wasn't going to let even a second slip away from me. For this challenge, we were allowed to bring in an outline or sketch of our finished scenes, and I gave my design a final glance before weighing out my flour. I'd painstakingly written out each stage with the complicated measurements, and I was so relieved to have them in front of me right now. It was the only way I could ignore the churning in my gut and the icy fear that gripped me.

I began by making the cookie dough for my child figures, including Matilda and Bruce. I told myself to watch the scales as I measured and take each step slowly. I'd practiced, and I was confident about the balance of ingredients and technique.

Once the dough was mixed and I'd gotten over the cacophony of eight other people using a food processor at the same time, I was ready to roll it out. I heaved the huge lump of dough onto my floured work surface.

I really enjoyed this part of making biscuits. There was something I found soothing about the rolling motion. Plus, it also gave me a chance to look around the room. I knew that Florence and Maggie were seriously pulling out all the stops today. Maggie was making a picnic scene from one of Enid Blyton's books; Florence was creating the scene in *The Adventures of Pinocchio* where Geppetto finishes carving Pinocchio and the puppet boy comes to life. Both were super-cool ideas, and I loved that Florence was staying true to her roots by referencing one of the great Italian children's stories of all time. Although how she was going to construct a puppet out of a biscuit, I had no idea.

Once my dough was properly rolled flat, I began to carve out my kids for the cake-eating scene. For the children in the classroom, I used a special cookie cutter that I'd ordered from a niche baking store in London. They made excellent, lifelike shapes. But I was going to carve Matilda, Bruce, and Miss Trunchbull—the stars of the show—by hand. I only hoped that my drawing skills would impress the judges; otherwise I was taking a pretty big risk. There were so many elements that could go wrong here, and I couldn't afford any silly mistakes.

Of course, this was exactly the moment that Elspeth came to talk to me. Elspeth wanted me to do well, I could *feel* it. It was just a shame that two cameras were following her and now training their lenses on me and my dough.

"Poppy," Elspeth said warmly, "I know you're making a scene from Roald Dahl's *Matilda*. Could you tell me what drew you to this book in particular and what flavors you're employing to bring it all to life?"

I took a breath and dived into my story about being read the book as a kid. I described the Philpotts' bakery and how the only thing that would settle my friends and me was story time. And we never tired of having *Matilda* read to us.

As I talked, I realized the other––now glaring––reason I'd been drawn to Matilda as a kid. She had special powers, misunderstood by those around her. I almost smacked my palm to my forehead: How could I have not seen the similarities between Matilda and me before? Of course, I couldn't do anything as cool as move objects around with my eyes, but I could see ghosts. And now I knew I was a water witch, other powers were starting to appear.

Elspeth thanked me and wished me luck before moving on to Amara, where Jonathon was quietly grilling her.

Amara was very nervous. She'd been explaining her biscuit scene to Jonathon but kept stumbling over the words. Now she was repeating the whole thing, but with a raised voice, almost shouting her explanation. I couldn't have blocked it out, even if I wanted to. "I chose *Little Women* as my book," she was saying. "I loved it so much as a kid, and I think I've reread it dozens of times. One of my favorite scenes is where Jo, one of the 'little women,' is wrapped in a blanket, sitting on an old sofa, eating apples and crying over *The Heir of Redclyffe.*"

I smiled to myself as I began to construct the gingerbread table on which I'd balance Bruce Bogtrotter's giant cookie-cake. I'd also loved *Little Women* when I was younger, especially the feisty character of Jo. Although each showstopper was unique, I liked how some of us had chosen to base our scene around food in books.

"I can't say I've read *Little Women* myself," Jonathon admitted, "but I can own up to reading a good book on the sofa munching apples, although more often it's a slice of apple strudel. Or tarte tatin."

"How about apple crumble?" Arty offered.

"Now you're talking," Jonathon said, blue eyes twinkling. "Apple crumble with thick pouring cream."

Arty pulled a face. "You have to eat apple crumble with lashings of hot custard," he said.

Jonathon shook his head playfully. "You couldn't be more wrong."

Arty turned and addressed the rest of the bakers. "Okay, everyone, important baking stuff here. Put down your tools for thirty seconds and answer me this riddle."

Was Arty serious right now? As if anyone had a spare thirty seconds. I looked around, trying to disguise my despair. Everyone reluctantly followed the instructions and halted their baking, although no one had managed to actually 'put down tools.' Instead we were firmly gripping rolling pins, wooden spoons, and cookie cutters as if our lives depended on it. Which they kind of did.

"Raise your hands if you think apple crumble is best with pouring cream?"

A few wooden spoons shot into the air.

"Now who thinks it's best with custard?"

One rolling pin and a sheet of baking paper went up.

Uh-oh. I hadn't voted on either.

Elspeth smiled and then cleared her throat. "And hands up for the people who know that the only answer to this question is apple crumble served with a giant scoop of Cornish vanilla ice cream."

I raised my hand, grinning. I loved it when Elspeth got

the last word. *And* she was right. Ice cream was by far the best option.

Arty shook his head playfully. "What a disgrace, the lot of you."

Despite the unwelcome interruption, Arty's little game had gone a long way to ease the tension in the tent. Everyone returned to the job at hand with looser shoulders, and if we weren't exactly smiling, at least our frown lines weren't stretching from here to Timbuktu.

After saying a quick wish-you-well to my people-shaped cookies, I slipped them into the oven. Now it was time to set about making the walls of the room, and then my oversize triple-chocolate cookie sandwich with chocolate buttercream filling to represent the cake. *So not much work left then.*

I kept my head down and got on with the second batch of dough. Jonathon was interviewing Hamish, and his Scottish accent boomed across the tent.

"I'm making a scene from Wallace and Gromit. I know it was an animation first, but I read the books to my two sweet nieces every time I see them. They love it."

"Isn't that nice?" Jilly said, butting in. "It's good to see a man not afraid of showing his sensitive side." Her blue glasses were pushed back into her hair, and her eyelashes were coated in thick layers of dark mascara.

At that, I stole a glance at Arty to see how he'd react to this mild flirtation, but he was busy torturing Euan, who was trying to construct an elaborate tree for Winnie-the-Pooh to lean against and eat a pot of honey. He was using a mix of vanilla, oats, nuts, and (of course) honey for his base.

"I'm making almost two hundred individual biscuits for this beauty," Euan said to Arty. "Have I been too ambitious?

Definitely. The sweat is on right now. This is more difficult than maneuvering around two hundred of my own bees."

"I think you might have stung yourself there, Euan." Arty chortled.

"Well, let's hope it's more honeypot than sting operation," Euan joked back.

I giggled to myself, but I couldn't let myself get distract-ed—Elspeth was already calling the halftime mark.

I switched off the food processor and scooped out the dough, ready to roll my next batch. I needed to get this into the oven and then on to making my buttercream pronto. Not to mention whipping up some icing, dyeing it different colors, then piping it onto the cookies to make different faces and hairstyles. Oh, man, I'd almost made this as tough for myself as Euan. But at least I could console myself knowing that I wasn't as up against it as Euan. Two hundred biscuits? That man was a glutton for punishment!

The second half of our allotted time flew by. I only looked up when my poor neck went into spasm from concentrating so hard. The third batch of my biscuits took longer to cook than I'd anticipated, and I was panicked about having enough time to let them cool before I iced them.

I erected my classroom walls and was beginning to arrange all the students when Jilly told us we had ten minutes left. My heart almost leapt straight out of my chest in fear. Was I going to be able to pull this one off? I couldn't have another bad bake.

I worked double-quick, arranging the giant triple-choco-late-chip cookie in the center of my room, and then squirted some chocolate frosting to attach Miss Trunchbull, Bruce, and Matilda. I watched my hands fly over my biscuity diorama almost as if they belonged to someone else. Sweat trickled down my neck.

When Jilly rang the final clanger, I stood back from the table and took a few deep breaths. I'd done it.

We brought our showstoppers to the table, and what a sight they were! I couldn't believe how inventive everyone had been. The combined skill was blowing my mind. Four hours of biscuit torture, and now we had to watch as the judges cracked into our scenes and destroyed them! Cruel or what?

I was so nervous, I could barely concentrate on the judging as Elspeth kicked off with Maggie's masterpiece. Words like "lovely lemon flavor...gorgeous texture...crumbly, buttery goodness" floated my way as the judging continued. But when they got to Euan's, I couldn't help but pay proper attention as Elspeth wrinkled her nose a little.

"Euan, I'm afraid you might have compromised taste for ambition," she said. "It's certainly impressive to look at, but the majority of your biscuits are far too thick and a little clumsy. There's much too much icing on here." Elspeth held up a piece of Winnie-the-Pooh, who now had his ear missing. "Look at that biscuit to icing ratio," she said, shaking her head a little.

"Not the best piping," Jonathon agreed.

Oh, poor Euan. This was *not* what you wanted to hear after hours of baking.

But then it was my turn.

"This looks very impressive, Poppy," Jonathon said.

"Yes, the whole composition is a triumph...even if that buttercream is oozing out of its cookie sandwich," Elspeth said, breaking off a piece of Trunchbull's "cake."

I held my breath as she bit into the chocolaty goo.

"Oh, how utterly rich and naughty. This is a delight."

I grinned. A delight!

But as Jonathon tried my vanilla biscuit people, he didn't appear to be as impressed. "These are a little overdone, Poppy."

My stomach sank into my shoes.

"But the flavor is excellent nonetheless."

I sighed in relief, but that was a silly mistake on my part. How could I have left them in the oven too long? Was my wishing-well prayer not loud enough or something?

Amara's nerves hadn't stopped her from turning out a really wonderful scene. And both Jonathon and Elspeth had rave reviews for her scene from *Little Women*.

When it was time for the results, I gripped my hands together. Florence, Amara, and Maggie were definitely all safe. Hamish's biscuit book had been widely praised. I knew I was teetering on the edge, as were Daniel and Priscilla. Euan had definitely received the worst feedback. I told myself that if I was sent home, it wouldn't be the end of the world. I would be a good sport and try really hard not to cry on camera.

After their deliberations, Elspeth and Jonathon agreed that Amara had won the showstopper challenge. She looked stunned and so happy I got a lump in my throat. Euan's was the worst and I'd moved up at least, to fourth place.

Next we were told who was going home. I knew I hadn't performed as well as I'd wanted to, so I held my breath, bracing myself to stave off those tears if they rushed into my eyes.

"Everyone today really pulled the stops out," Arty said. "You made an amazing effort, bakers, but sadly, we do have to send someone home. And this week we're going to say goodbye to our very lovable beekeeper Euan," he continued in a grave voice. "You've been an absolute pleasure to have on the show, mate. And you've made some sterling bakes. You should be very proud of yourself."

Euan looked gutted. As a group, we naturally divided so that half of us comforted Euan and the other half congratulated Amara and then switched.

Inside, I was saying a private thank-you to the biscuit gods for being on my side today. I was safe for another week.

CHAPTER 18

$\mathcal{B}$ack at the inn, the whole gang tumbled into the pub totally exhausted. We were spent and thirsty for something to take the edge off. I lingered by the entrance, reluctant to get into the spirit of things.

On our walk back from the tent, something shocking had occurred to me. The moment that I was free to think about something other than cookie dough, my mind had raced back to Eileen, the letter, and her horrible nephew. While we'd been busy baking, it had started raining outside, and the late-afternoon air smelled like clay. I let the others walk on ahead. A few thin, straight trees were growing in a line next to each other, and I took a seat on a log beside them, not caring about the drizzle.

I still couldn't get my head around why Eileen's last words would be about a letter. If she was referring to the letter from Oliver Jones, then where was it? If only I knew more about this Oliver chap. What was his life like in Canada? Was he married now? Who would tell him his childhood friend was dead? A missing letter from a missing boy. It was such a puzzle. All I knew about Oliver was what Bill and Barbara had said about him being unhappy at home, that he and Penelope were competitive siblings and Eileen had possibly had a crush on him.

But as the rain trickled through the umbrella of leaves and landed on me in cool, light droplets, I tried to let thought go and simply let impressions come to me.

I was still there when Florence stuck her head around the pub's door and told me off for being slow. "Come on, Poppy," she called. "Don't be a party pooper. You're safe! We're safe! And we don't have to look at another biscuit for as long as we live!"

I laughed. "I'll drink to that."

The gang had commandeered the biggest table in the pub, and Gaurav was beaming. Euan was being a good sport, telling everyone who'd listen that he was happy to have made it as far as he had and he wouldn't mind a lie-in next weekend. I watched the scene almost as if I were an outsider to it all. I couldn't shake my heavy heart. At least Eve's smiling face was behind the bar. Maybe she could answer some of the difficult questions I had.

Amara saw me then and thrust a champagne flute in my hand. "Today deserves a proper toast."

"Congratulations, Amara," I said. "Your book was beautiful. You deserved to win." We clinked, and I took a sip, letting the bubbles burst pleasantly in my mouth.

But my moment of peace was brief. A man, clearly already a little inebriated, was talking loudly at the bar. I looked up and saw to my horror that Timothy, Eileen's nephew, was the drunk in question. Oh, man. What was the brute doing here? And why was he drunk? Hadn't the police been to question him today?

I leaned over and whispered in Florence's ear. "That's the guy who nearly ran me over yesterday."

"What?" she exclaimed. "I'm going straight over to give that idiot a piece of my mind!" Her chair scraped across the pub's tile floor.

I laid a hand on her arm. "Please don't. I want to go and see what he's wittering on about. Let me stay incognito for a minute."

Florence pouted but agreed, and I excused myself from the table and slipped over to the bar so I could better hear that buffoon.

Eve was being incredibly patient as she poured Timothy a pint of bitter.

"The bloody cheek of them," he was saying. "Questioning *me* about *my* whereabouts." He was red-faced. "Whereyouhavebeen?" he said, slurring a little and mimicking Sgt. Lane's voice. I had a sudden desire to defend poor Adam Lane, but I had to hold my tongue. I needed to see what else Timothy was going to spill.

"They seemed to think I was in Broomewode yesterday, but I kept telling them I was in London. Apparently an 'eyewitness'"—he made air quotes with his crooked red fingers—"saw me driving in the village." He shook his head angrily. "I drove up as soon as I heard the news. And I was at Aunt Eileen's cottage, having a clear-out, when they almost knocked my door down. Talk about disrespectful."

"You mean Eileen's door," Eve said softly. "They almost knocked down Eileen's door."

"Exactly. Anyway, they kept asking me about a stupid

calendar my aunt was supposed to have in the kitchen and did I know where it might be. I mean, what kind of trip are these coppers on, asking me about a calendar?"

Just then my phone buzzed, and a text message appeared from a number I didn't recognize.

I opened the notification and saw that it was Ophelia. Despite myself, I grinned. *The* Lady Ophelia was texting *me*.

POPPY, Ophelia here. After our meeting this morning, I did a bit of digging. It turns out that Eileen and Benedict have the same solicitor. I called in a little favor, and the lawyer confirmed that Eileen had an appointment but wouldn't say anything further...despite my best efforts. I've passed the information to the police. Thought you might like to know.
O X

WOW. I felt my mouth drop open. Ophelia had come to the rescue again. But if Timothy had found out that Eileen might be changing her will had that make him angry enough to meddle with Eileen's medication? Had he upset her so much she had a heart attack and died? And which of them had shoved her will in the cutlery drawer?

"Anyway, enough about me. I'm here to honor my lovely aunt Eileen," Timothy said. He spun round and faced the room. "Who's going to join me in a toast? I'm paying, of course. Let's have ourselves a little wake, shall we?"

Behind him, Eve wrinkled her nose in disgust. I caught her eye and shook my head. This was *not* how you honored a person. Eileen deserved a proper wake; her loved ones needed to tell stories about her life, share their lovely memories and pay reverence to all the qualities she embodied. There was nothing respectful about an inebriated family member offering some strangers a free pint.

I guessed that everyone shared my sentiments, because the room was completely silent. I turned and looked back over at my fellow bakers. They were clearly uncomfortable—Florence was practically squirming in her chair, so desperate was she to give Timothy a piece of her mind. And from Maggie's frown, Florence had obviously shared my near-miss with Timothy's car. That's when I spied Susan and Reg in the far corner, looking pretty cozy over a bottle of red wine. Their eyes were fixed on Timothy and not without judgment, either.

The room stayed silent.

"All right, then, let me drink alone. See if I care," Timothy muttered.

I stayed by the bar, watching Timothy grumble into his pint.

I was halfway back to the table when Penelope walked into the pub. She was wearing a black skirt and long-sleeved top with a high neck. As soon as I saw her, something in my mind clicked, and I knew what it was that had been bothering me. But now I had to prove it. My stomach churned as I watched her take a seat next to Timothy.

"Are you all right, Poppy?" Gaurav asked. "You look like you've seen a ghost."

Oh, man, if I had a dollar, or a pound, for every time I had actually seen a ghost, I'd be a very rich woman.

"Hmm, I recognize that look," Hamish said. "What are you up to, Poppy?"

"I'm okay," I murmured. "I have a hunch about something. And if I'm right, well...I don't want to be right. Do you see what I'm saying?"

"The mysterious Poppy strikes again," Florence said. "No one knows what you're saying, darling."

Instead of answering, I watched the ease with which Penelope accepted a red wine from Timothy. She raised her glass. "To my best friend, Eileen. She's in a better place now, smiling down on all of us, I'm sure."

Hmmm, I wasn't so sure about that myself.

Penelope's toast broke the silent spell that had been cast over the pub, for everyone raised their glass, too. "To Eileen," the room chimed in unison, clinking glasses.

It was a touching moment. But one I knew I had to shatter.

And as if I'd magically summoned them—had I magically summoned them? I'd have to ask Elspeth about that one. I saw DI Hembly and Sgt. Lane enter the pub and speak to Eve. I took a deep breath and approached Penelope and Timothy. I wondered if he'd remember my face.

"Poppy, dear," Penelope said, smiling. "I'm so glad you're here. Can I get you a drink?"

I shook my head at the offer of a drink. Timothy was looking at me curiously. Clearly he remembered my face, but he couldn't place it.

"But it would be nice to talk more about Eileen," I said. "There's been something playing on my mind, and I can't work it out."

Penelope looked puzzled. "I'm not sure if I can help you, but I'll certainly try."

Out of the corner of my eye, I caught DI Hembly raise an

eyebrow. But neither he nor Sgt. Lane interrupted me. I hoped that was because they could now spot when my sleuth instincts were kicking in. So far, my hunches had been right. But that didn't mean I couldn't be wrong.

"Yesterday, we talked about Eileen and Oliver exchanging letters."

"Yes, that's right."

"And I told you that Eileen was trying to tell me something important before she died. Something about a letter."

Penelope nodded, but looked around as though hoping for someone else to talk to.

"But when I was having tea at Eileen's house, going through old photographs, she showed me her stacks of correspondence." Okay, that was a white lie but I thought Eileen would approve. "She kept every letter she ever received. But you know, I never saw one from Oliver Jones. Which is strange, don't you think? Why would he only contact her now, decades after he left for Canada?"

Penelope drew herself up tightly. "I don't think it's nice to bring up the past this way. Eileen was devastated when Oliver left. I don't think she'd want us going over old ground again. She's barely cold. Have some respect."

A chair scraped back, and Hamish came to join me. In his softest voice, Hamish said, "Let her talk."

"What business is it of hers? She barely knew Eileen," Penelope challenged.

Timothy swiveled on his barstool and leaned forward and stared at me. "I know your face. You're—" He was about to say where he recognized me from but stopped himself just in time.

I glared at Timothy, then turned back to Penelope. This was it.

"I don't buy it. There's no way your brother would contact Eileen out of the blue like that. She was very distressed when she received that letter."

The color was draining from Penelope's face. "I'm sure there had been other letters. Eileen must have thrown them away."

Hamish spoke up. "But kept every other letter she ever received?" He shook his head. "That doesn't sound likely."

All I had was a theory. But so far my instincts had been right, and Penelope was looking decidedly uncomfortable. I shot a look over at DI Hembly, and Sgt. Lane gave me a small nod. Okay, if I had the confidence of those two, then surely I could do this. I took a deep breath, realizing that the pub was still silent and everyone was watching me, waiting to see what I was about to say.

"I was looking at old photographs with Eileen, and she gave me one to keep. You were in it and Bill and Barbara—you recall them? Well, they recognized you immediately, and they were the first ones to tell me about Oliver going missing. They also happened to mention how you and Oliver fought a lot as kids. I was surprised that they remembered that because all siblings fight. I guess the two of you must have made a real impression."

Penelope crossed her arms. "We were just ordinary siblings. Squabbling and play-fighting. I'm not sure why you'd bring that up now when I've lost my best friend." She made a sound like a sob and pulled out a handkerchief from where it was tucked up her sleeve, dabbing her eyes.

"I think that one day, your play-fighting got a little too real. What happened?"

Penelope swallowed. She was white, and as she wiped her cheeks I could see her hands were trembling. I had her exactly where I wanted her. "Stop this."

Instead of backing way I pushed. I really hoped I was right or I was going to feel truly terrible about what I was doing. "And Eileen was somehow involved," I continued. "Did she see you?"

There was a silence that seemed to stretch into eternity. *Hold your ground, Poppy. Stay firm. You've got this.*

"That's...that's the most preposterous thing I've ever heard," Penelope finally spluttered.

Exactly what I thought she'd say.

I slipped my phone from my back pocket. "Here you go then," I said, handing over the phone. "Why don't you give Oliver a call?"

Penelope stared at the phone.

"Go ahead. Vancouver is eight hours behind us. He'll be having his morning coffee. Maybe sailing or climbing up a mountain, whatever they do in Vancouver. So happy to hear from his only sister."

DI Hembly and Sgt. Lane stepped forward from the shadows.

Penelope looked from them to me and back again. She checked her watch. "My brother and I aren't close. Anyway, today is about Eileen."

DI Hembly cleared his throat. "We've had Vancouver police searching for Oliver Jones. They're having trouble locating him."

The silence in the room deepened. I could see Penelope's

brain working overtime, desperately searching for a way out, for a plausible excuse. I kept my face as expressionless as I could manage. But Penelope was struggling to do the same. It was now or never. I took a deep breath and stabbed her with my words. "Oliver never left Broomewode, did he, Penelope? Because you killed him."

CHAPTER 19

*I*nto the stunned silence, Penelope let out a short burst of angry laughter and looked around the room as if to say *Who is this joker?* "How dare you? I've never heard anything so absurd. The police searched every inch of our family home and the surrounding property. Search parties were sent out. No trace of Oliver was ever found."

"You didn't deny killing him," I said.

Her face looked waxy and her hands gripped themselves into fists, the wet hankie trailing like a drooping tail. "Of course, I deny it. If your crazed theory is correct, then where are Oliver's remains?"

"Buried beneath the rose bush in Eileen's back garden," I answered promptly.

Someone gasped. Possibly Timothy. Penelope's mouth began to tremble. There was a long pause. "Did Eileen tell you?"

I shook my head. "No. I was in her back garden, sketching the beautiful roses, when I saw the plaque next to the bush. It said: *To nurture a garden is to feed not just the body, but the soul.*

And as I read it, a cool breeze went down my spine. There was something about that dedication that stayed with me. I didn't know it at the time, but that cool breeze, well, I think it was Oliver's soul."

Penelope shook her head rapidly from side to side. "No, no. This is madness," she said, but tears spilled over again.

"Penelope?" Timothy asked, putting down his pint. "I don't understand."

The tears slid down her face, forming tracks down her powdered cheeks. There was a long silence until finally Penelope opened her mouth and a tiny voice came out. "It was all an accident. A terrible accident. I never meant to do it. We were just playing. It was a pillow fight. And it got out of control. We were both so stubborn, both in love with winning. And Oliver was always trying to overpower me. He was stronger. But I managed to get a strong hold on him. I held the pillow over his face, waiting for him to admit I'd won, but he wouldn't. After a while he stopped struggling, but I thought he was pretending to be still so I'd take the pillow away and he'd jump on me." She gasped, and a keening sound came from her mouth. "But he wasn't pretending. I couldn't wake him up.." She broke into a sob. "I never meant to do it. It was an accident. But I was only a young girl, and I was scared."

A collective gasp rippled through the room.

I nodded. "But you weren't the only one who was scared, were you?"

Penelope stopped crying, sat up straight, and her voice was suddenly calm. "I don't know what you mean."

"Eileen was with you."

"So she *did* tell you."

I shook my head. "She didn't breathe a word to anyone. But she was getting to the end of her life. Did she want to finally tell the truth before she passed away? You weren't going to let that happen, were you?"

There was a sudden crash, and Timothy's pint splashed over the rim of his glass. "Penny," he said, aghast. "You were Auntie Eileen's best friend."

"That's what I thought, Timothy," Penelope said. "But true friends don't turn their back on each other. And that's exactly what Eileen was going to do."

Penelope turned to face me again. "Eileen helped me bury Oliver. We knew no one would look at the bottom of Eileen's parents' garden. We were in it together. We got shovels from her father's shed and we dug a hole and buried my brother. We agreed we'd never speak of it to anyone."

"Then last week I went to Eileen's cottage for tea and I saw the solicitor's appointment on her calendar. I knew that Eileen had updated her will only last year, so I asked her what it was about. And that's when she told me that her heart condition had been getting worse. Her doctor said she wouldn't survive surgery. Before she died, she said she wanted to put things right and thought that Oliver deserved to finally have a proper funeral and burial. She didn't want to die with that secret on her conscience."

"But it was your secret, too."

She nodded. "She'd left her cottage to Timothy, and she knew that if he decided to sell it to a developer or did any landscaping, then they'd unearth the remains buried in her garden. She couldn't bear it. She told me our secret had ruined her life. She was never able to move because Oliver was buried there, and she'd never married because of the guilt and fear of one day being found out. So she was going to the solicitor to find out what she and I could do to admit to the crime without ending up in jail."

"Oh, you'd have gone to jail," Hamish assured her. "The law requires we pay for our crimes."

I continued, "So you sent her a letter from Oliver. I saw it on her kitchen table the day she received it."

Penelope nodded slowly.

"What a cruel thing to do."

"It might seem that way to you, but I couldn't have Eileen ruin everything. There was no need to dig up the past. What was done was done. So I sent her the letter from Oliver as a warning. I knew she'd understand. I wrote as though he'd lived a long, happy life. That's how I wanted her to think of him."

"That letter brought on an attack of angina, Penelope. She was pale and frightened and in pain. You did that to your best friend."

Penelope screwed up her face. "Oh, poor Eileen," she said, her voice thick with sarcasm. "Always the victim. She played that part all her life." Her expression soured further, and deep rivets ran across her forehead. "But she was guilty too. She was there; she saw what happened and she didn't stop me from killing my own brother. Why didn't she stop me?"

I pictured Eileen as a child, either speechless with fright, or trying to get Penelope to stop and being ignored.

"Easier to blame it all on me. When I told her she was just being a silly old woman, worrying herself about the past, she had the nerve to say I frightened her. That I'd always frightened her and our whole friendship had been bound by this terrible secret, nothing more."

Penelope's breath came out in little bursts, and then tears began to stream down her face again. "How could she say that?"

"And because she hurt your feelings, you killed her. And then your secret would be safe forever."

"I can't believe it," Timothy said, looking at her in horror. "I've known you my whole life, Penny. How could you?"

DI Hembly and Sgt. Lane stepped forward.

"What did you do to Eileen, Penelope?" DI Hembly asked her.

She glanced at him and then down. "I knew where Eileen kept her heart medication, so I crushed some of her pills. I dropped into the shop that afternoon and made us both tea. I stirred the crushed medication into her tea. I knew the dose would be toxic. And it killed her."

Sergeant Lane got out his handcuffs. Penelope looked at them and said, "Eileen managed to ruin me anyway, even from the grave."

He read her her rights and I bowed my head as Penelope was led away. I didn't want to be a witness to any more pain.

I was also experiencing some heart pangs of my own. I'd jumped to conclusions again and suspected Susan Bentley of foul play just because she knew about the medicinal qualities of foxgloves. I looked over to where she and Reginald were sitting. Susan raised her glass and mouthed, "To Eileen." I smiled back and vowed to be more trustful of my coven sister. But the jury was still out about Reg. After what Edward had said about his blacksmithing, that made Reg a fraud in my books.

"I can't believe it," Timothy said, watching Penelope being led away.

"I nearly accused you of murder," I told him.

"Me?" He stood up all innocent and full of righteous indignation.

"You were in Broomewode yesterday. I know because you nearly ran me over with your car. Why did you lie?"

He looked as though he'd deny it again, but it was pretty clear that everyone in the pub was on my side and no one on his. He got all huffy and said, "Fine. I was in Broomewode. If you must know, I asked to borrow money from my aunt. I got myself into a bit of a tight spot, that's all."

"And did she give it to you?"

His mouth was very little for his big, red face, and now it pinched even smaller, like a baby's. "No. No. She didn't. Said it was time I stood on my own two feet."

Good for you, Eileen, I thought. He stared into his drink. "I was angry. I may have said a few things I'll always regret." He looked as though he might cry. "But she knew I loved her." He suddenly glanced up at me as though I were judge and jury. "She had to know I loved her and didn't mean it."

And that, I thought, would be his punishment. If he had any conscience at all, he'd suffer for the way he treated her on her last day on earth. Maybe he hadn't caused her heart failure—that had been Penny—but he'd hurt her heart.

Hamish laid his hand on mine and led me back to the group, who were all staring.

"Blimey, Poppy," Maggie whispered. "You haven't half got the knack for cracking a murder case."

"And one that's been cold for years and years," Hamish added, whistling through his teeth.

"You did rather upstage my win," Amara said, handing me back my glass of fizz. "I think you deserve this more than me."

I shook my head but smiled. I'd taken a risk by airing my theory, but I'd been right. At first, I'd thought Eileen's death was natural, but after Timothy lied about being in Broomewode, I'd begun to question everything.

Slowly, the pub came back to life, and sounds of conversation and merriment filled the room.

"I think it's about time we gave a proper toast to Eileen, don't you?" Hamish said, his voice warm with affection.

We all raised our glasses in the air.

"To Eileen," I said. "A generous and forgiving lady. May she rest in peace."

CHAPTER 20

Ophelia texted me again the next morning congratulating me on catching a murderer. She said the earl and Lady Frome had invited me to Broomewode Hall before lunch to sketch the interiors. I knew she'd made that invitation happen and I was grateful to her all over again.

A big smile spread across my face, and my stomach began to turn somersaults. "What do you think about that, huh?" I asked Gateau.

For once, she looked supportive and mewed her approval.

"I'm finally going to be able to see that oil painting up close. After all this time, after all those thwarted plans. All it took was befriending a famous humanitarian doctor. Who knew?"

I leapt out of bed and into the shower, desperate to haul ass to the manor house.

A few of the bakers who didn't have work on Monday had stayed an extra night at the inn, exhausted after yesterday's epic showstopper, but I hoped I was up early enough to skip seeing them at breakfast. I wanted to slip away unnoticed and avoid having to explain where I was going so early.

I got dressed quickly in my new denim skirt and a white T-shirt, dragged a brush through my tangled hair until it was smooth, and slipped my feet into my running shoes. The birds chirped through my open window, and as I flung back the curtains, I saw that yesterday's cloudy weather had disappeared and blue skies had returned with fervor.

"Are you coming with?" I asked Gateau. "You could stretch those paws of yours in the gardens."

She leapt up and trotted over to the door.

I laughed. "Okay, okay. I'm coming. Let me just tie this lace."

I was about to leave when a familiar figure floated back through the door.

"Hello, Gerry. Impeccable timing, as always."

Gateau hissed and leapt back on the bed.

Gerry scowled at her. "Going out, are you? Well, I only came to congratulate you on another mystery solved. You're on a roll, Poppy Wilkinson. The spirit world is all the better off for having you—well, if not *in* it, then near it. You're like a cheerleader for the departed. No crime against a spirit left unsolved."

"A cheerleader." I laughed. "Believe me, helping to send someone to prison does not feel like a pep rally."

Gerry waved some imaginary pom-poms in the air.

"You did great, Pops. But make sure you don't let all this affect your baking. You've been slipping down the ranks."

I hung my head. I knew what he was saying was right, but I hated that it was so obvious.

Gerry could see he'd hit a raw nerve. "You're a real baking

talent. Just make sure to show 'em what you're made of next week."

I agreed but told Gerry I had to dash.

"Yes, yes, I know. You're busy. Always busy."

Gerry gave a high five his best shot, then floated through the door. "Until next week," he called from the hallway.

I picked up Gateau, and together we raced down to the pub. I grabbed a blueberry muffin then hot-footed out of there before anyone saw me.

As we walked to Broomewode Hall, I couldn't get my racing heart to settle. I was hoping beyond hope that Ophelia would be the one to answer the door and I could avoid the earl and Lady Frome entirely. I was sure that Lord Frome would have forgotten all about his offer for me to sketch the interiors of his house, and Lady Frome hadn't even tried to mask her horror at the idea. There was something about the haughty figure of Lady Frome that aroused my suspicions, but I'd yet to figure it out. What I did know was that getting in her bad books was *not* something I wanted to do. I was going to have to be very careful once I'd crossed the threshold of that house.

The Georgian manor house loomed before me, golden and imposing in the morning sun. Its symmetrical windows appeared to me as unblinking, all-seeing eyes. The turrets reached proudly up into the blue sky. On my left was the ornamental lake, the swans floating serene and elegant on its surface. I stopped and turned toward the lake. I stayed there for a moment, watching the water's surface intently, hoping that another vision would appear and tell me that I was on the right path or at least that I was getting closer to discovering more about my birth family. But the only ripples that appeared came from a pair of ducks bobbing for food.

I turned back onto the main path and soon reached the carriage drive. I had such high hopes pinned on today's visit. Getting into that dining room and studying the painting had become an obsession.

So I took a deep, steadying breath, stepped into the portico entrance, and faced the front door with my head held high. I remembered to pull the thick red rope hanging from a circular brass plate rather than use the imposing lion's head knocker. A crashing bell joined the sound of birds tweeting, and I suddenly felt very, very nervous.

The bell reverberated through the long entrance hall for what seemed like an eternity. I waited for the sound of footsteps and tried to ignore the two tiny cameras hidden in the ivy that graced the top of the portico. What if the Champneys were watching me on camera and instructed their butler not to open the door?

But my worries were quelled when it finally swung open and there was Ophelia's smiling face.

"Poppy!" she said. "So glad you could make it."

As if I wouldn't give my prized mixer to be here.

"Come in, come in," she continued, ushering me into the vast hallway. She was dressed more formally than I'd seen before, in an off-white linen suit. Her long blond hair had been pulled into a sleek ponytail, and there were tiny pearls in her ears. I could see Tilbury, the butler, hovering in the background, a mortified expression on his face.

Ophelia whispered into my ear, "He's cross because I refused to let him answer the door. I'm perfectly capable of turning a handle myself."

I smiled weakly and asked if she'd slept well.

"Oh yes, I sleep like a baby. Honestly, not even close-range gunfire can wake me up. It's a hazard." She laughed her demure, soft laugh and then made me fill her in on all the details of the drama in the pub last night.

"I'm so sorry I missed it, but I'm delighted I got to know you. You have quite the reputation around here for solving mysteries," she said. "Clearly you have brilliant instincts about people. But you care about people. That's why you've such good detective skills. You care."

I was sure that I was beetroot red. The great humanitarian Ophelia Wren was complimenting me? I could only mumble my thanks, humbled by her kind words.

"Have you any thoughts on where you'd like to start sketching? The earl and Lady Frome are still in the breakfast room, so I hope you don't mind that they haven't come down to greet you."

I shook my head quickly. Maybe a little too fast. The farther from those two I could keep, the better. And, of course, I knew exactly where I'd like to start sketching. "The dining room, I've heard it's an excellent example of the, um, period." I wished I'd had more time to research Georgian architecture so I could sound like I had a clue what I was talking about.

"Come this way, and we'll get you set up."

Ophelia led me along the hallway, lit by the dusty-looking chandelier I'd noticed last time I was here. The paneled walls seemed to suck up any light that came in through the leaded windows. I spotted the suit of armor in the corner and the long ottoman where I'd sat waiting for Lady Frome. The pungent scent of lilies filled my nose.

Finally, Ophelia opened a door on the right hand, and we walked into the dining room.

I inhaled sharply. I'd gone over the details of this room so many times that it felt as familiar to me as my own bedroom.

There were the enormous bay windows, framed by heavy tapestried curtains woven through with gold. The cream-wallpapered walls reached up to the paneled ceilings, which were bordered by a deep red runner. The ancient-looking long dining table was a rich mahogany color, which matched the sideboards and display cabinets. The damask-uphol-stered chairs were much larger than I'd thought from seeing them on TV.

And there, hanging by the window in the left-hand corner, was the painting itself. I had to clench my fists into little balls to fight the urge to run straight to it. But I had to keep my composure for Ophelia's sake. As much as I was grateful to her, I couldn't let the real reason I was here become apparent. What would I do if she stayed to keep me company?

But I needn't have worried, as Ophelia said, "I wish I could stick around and watch you work, but I've got a lunch meeting in London." She checked her watch. "I'd better get a move-on. Ben knows you're here. Make sure to tell me how it goes later? You've got my number." And then, to my total surprise, she rushed over, air-kissed my cheeks and gave me a warm wave as she elegantly strode toward the door.

I couldn't wait a second longer and rushed over to the oil painting. Like the chairs, it was much larger than I thought, and the colors were richer, full of depth. I rummaged in my bag and pulled out my sketchbook. Inside was the photo-graph that Eileen had given me. I looked from the painting to the photo. It was definitely the same woman, the same shawl. Thanks to Eileen, I now knew that the grand woman sitting in the wicker chair was the previous viscount's mother and her name was Elizabetta.

She was beautiful. Her light-brown hair was pulled up in an old-fashioned style so that a few strands curled at the edges of her face. Her eyes were greenish-gray and smiling so that they creased a little in the corners. Her lips were painted a soft, natural peach, and her cheeks were flushed to match. If Eileen hadn't told me that she'd been a kind lady, I would have seen it captured by the softness of her expression. It seemed to invite you to spill all your secrets.

And there was her woolen shawl. My baby blanket. Now that I was up close, I could say for certain that the pattern matched exactly. I exhaled deeply and realized that I'd been holding my breath all this time. I snapped a couple of photos with my phone.

But if I'd been hoping for an epiphany of some kind, then I was going to be kept waiting. Despite having the link between us confirmed, I was no closer to understanding why Elizabetta was wearing my baby blanket as a shawl. Was it the same blanket, or had the same person knitted both versions? It was hard to believe that such a complicated pattern could be replicated, but maybe it wouldn't be such a challenge for a master knitter.

I put my face as close as I could to the painting without it touching my nose. I kicked myself for not bringing my blanket with me this weekend. How I'd love to have it now so I could compare stitch for stitch.

I was still holding this inelegant position when I heard, "Good morning."

I spun round, and there was Benedict Champney wearing a bemused expression, hands on the hips of his jeans. Did he think I was planning to steal the artwork? Maybe stuff the sterling in my bag? I wondered if I'd be searched on my way out. "Oh, hello," I said as coolly as I could manage. Like my nose wasn't half an inch from one of his family portraits. "I was taken by this painting. It's very beautiful."

He came closer. "Ah, yes, Elizabetta. She was the Countess before mother. A cousin of ours. She died when I was very young, so I don't remember much about her, but the old staff still talk about her fondly."

I suddenly felt very sad. "She must have been a very kind woman. I think she gave that shawl away to a desperate young woman."

Benedict looked stern, suddenly, and I realized that I'd already given too much away. The Champneys were a private bunch, and Benedict wasn't going to respond well to me talking as if I was chummy with one of them.

"How on earth do you know that?" he asked. "You couldn't have been acquainted with Elizabetta. You're much too young."

"Oh, just village gossip."

He frowned again. "Well, village gossip tells me that you'd better get your head back in the game or you're not going to make it much further in the competition."

I stared at him, open-mouthed. He was right, of course, but I was shocked that he knew. Or cared.

Benedict gathered himself up until he stood ramrod-straight. "There's a bell on the ottoman in the hallway. When you're finished here, ring it, and Tilbury will see you out."

And without so much as a goodbye, Benedict turned on his heels and left.

But there was no need to subtly hustle me out. I'd seen what I came here for, and now I knew that the shawl in the painting was the exact match of my baby blanket. Elizabetta must have given it to my birth mother.

I went back to the painting. "But who are you? Why did you give a frightened young girl that shawl?" She must have prized it since she'd chosen to be painted in it.

Unfortunately, the smiling woman didn't answer, but as I stood there I felt a warmth hug around me, as though I'd been wrapped in a shawl.

CHAPTER 21

I decided to end my weekend where I'd started it: at Broomewode Farm. Even though Susan had no idea that I'd suspected she might be involved in Eileen's death, I felt pretty sheepish about jumping to conclusions. Susan had been generous and kind to me from the moment we first met, from her happy eggs and sharing her secret gooseberry plot to showing me the plants and herbs to use in magic tonics. It was just that darn Reginald. Their close friendship was still suspicious to my mind, and after what Edward, the gardener, revealed about those fireplace tools, I now knew for sure that Reg wasn't all that he presented to the world. But despite her dodgy taste in company, I wanted to say goodbye to Susan before I made the drive home. And maybe fit in a little ball-throwing for Sly, too.

Armed with my sketchbook, I left Broomewode Hall with a huge grin on my face, feeling thoroughly satisfied now that I'd finally seen the painting for myself. I turned left onto the path that led to the farm and enjoyed the warm sunshine and tweeting birds. For the first time all weekend, my mind was clear and calm. No murders to solve, no biscuits to bake.

Before long, Susan's glorious herb garden came into view, and I inhaled its earthy, fresh scent. And then the calm was shattered by a happy bark, and Sly almost knocked me over in his excitement.

"Hello, hello!" I called, laughing. "You don't know your own strength, you silly goof."

Sly barked again and used his nose to nudge his red ball toward me. I gave him a big stroke and picked up that slobbery ball, hurling it across the garden.

The side door to the farmhouse opened, and Susan emerged. My jaw almost dropped to the ground. I'd never seen Susan wearing anything but farming clothes: jodhpurs and gumboots and sensible waterproofs. But here she was in a long, pleated blue shirt with a billowy white smock. Her reddish curly crop had been brushed away from her face, and was that—yes, she was wearing blush on her cheeks. And a spot of lipstick too.

"Susan!" I called out. "You look fabulous."

She beamed and came toward me. "I needed to do something to raise my spirits." She held the folds of her skirt and then let it drop. "Isn't it pretty?" she asked.

"Gorgeous."

"We're off for a drive. Reg has ordered me to stop working so hard. We're heading into Bath for lunch. I can't remember the last time I went into the city."

Of course Reg was behind this. But I couldn't begrudge his intentions. Susan looked happy.

As if on cue, a rumbling noise came from the side of the

house, and then a racing-green Morgan pulled up next to the farmhouse.

"He's into classic cars, you know," Susan said.

More than blacksmithing, that's for sure.

Reg stepped out of the car and came to join us. His thick mass of silver hair was swept back with a glossy gel, and he looked very smart in a green tweed suit, a white shirt open at the neck. Susan was beaming, and they greeted each other with a chaste kiss on the cheek.

But Edward's words about the tools were still ringing in my ears. *Whoever did this has been at his trade for years and years. Decades, probably. This isn't amateur stuff.*

"I suppose 'congratulations' might seem an odd word, but well done, you, for putting Penelope to rights last night," Reginald said.

"It was nothing," I replied, shrugging. "Just a hunch."

I had a hunch he wouldn't be too pleased when I told Susan he wasn't a classic-car-driving, blacksmithing hero. He was a fraud.

I was about to open my mouth and hope a more delicate way of expressing this sentiment came out, but the side door to the farmhouse opened again.

"I thought that was you, Poppy."

It was Edward, the gardener. He was wearing green trousers and a matching T-shirt with Broomewode Hall stitched in white thread.

I raised my eyebrows. "What are you doing here?"

Edward laughed and ran a hand through his thick hair. "Don't look so happy to see me."

"He's my new lodger," Susan explained.

Reg cleared his throat. "Since you may have already

cottoned on, Poppy, I'll admit that perhaps my blacksmithing skills weren't all I claimed them to be."

Susan linked his arm and patted him gently on the shoulder. "Proud, silly thing," she said.

Reg stared at his car keys rather than look at me. "I had high hopes for my skills as a blacksmith when I moved down here. Keen as mustard. With all the tools."

"All the gear, no idea." Susan laughed softly.

"Exactly. I wasn't good enough. But by the time I'd discovered that fact, I'd already promised Eileen some goods for the shop to boost sales. I'm embarrassed to admit I contracted a fine blacksmith in Scotland to turn out my pieces. I shouldn't have done it when the truth is, I'm still learning."

I turned to Susan. "You knew?"

"Oh, yes," she replied.

Reginald unlinked arms with Susan and clapped a hand on Edward's back. "But Edward here has agreed to train me in blacksmithing."

"And I'm going to teach Edward about beekeeping so that he can help me out with the hives," Susan said.

"Win-win," Edward said.

"Come on, you," Reg said to Susan. "We've got a reservation to keep."

I said my goodbyes and told Susan I'd be back next week. I was hoping for some more "happy eggs" to use in the next round which we'd been told was European Tradition. I was going to need a little extra oomph to get back into the judges' good books. Susan promised she'd set aside some eggs from her favorite hen (only Susan would have a favorite hen), and after a final ball throw for Sly, I turned and headed back toward the inn.

"Wait up," Edward called. "Let me grab my bag, and I'll walk with you."

We set off along the cobbled path that would take me back to the inn and Edward to work. As we walked, Edward told me how lucky he was to have found board with Susan. He'd been renting an expensive room in the next village and driving in, but now his commute was a pleasant fifteen-minute walk. He was glad to share his knowledge of black-smithing with Reginald; it would keep his skills in good shape.

"You don't mind that he lied?" I asked.

Edward shook his head. "I can understand why. Broomewode is a very closed community. They're not exactly welcoming to outsiders. I've seen that with the gardening team. Reginald just wanted to fit in. You can't blame a chap for that."

I supposed I'd had a lucky time being part of a coven. I really did appreciate having Eve and Susan here in Broomewode.

We reached the end of the path, and I said goodbye as Edward turned onto the grounds of Broomewode Hall. The vast white tent looked magnificent in the sunlight, and I promised myself that next time I was beneath that awning, I'd bake my little heart out.

As if she'd heard my promise, Elspeth emerged from the tent. I waved at her and waited until she reached me.

She looked more casual than when filming was in progress, comfortable in a pair of cream slacks and short-sleeved khaki shirt. Her silver hair hung freely in a neat, long bob. "Poppy," she said, smiling, "I thought I might have missed you. This morning's team meeting went on for ages."

She shrugged. "Donald Friesen is a thorough man. Anyway, I wanted to talk to you."

Oh no. Was I in trouble?

"Poppy, you've managed to stay away from physical danger this week, but now you're in danger of being sent home."

I snapped my head up and stared at Elspeth aghast. "Is the warning note right? Is someone trying to get me to leave the show? I was hoping it might just be a prank from one of the other contestants, but now I'm not so sure."

"No, dear," Elspeth said. "I'm trying to tell you to pull your baking socks up. You skated on thin ice this week, Poppy, and you need to do better next week if you want to stay on the show."

My heart sank into my shoes. I hated that I'd let Elspeth down. I'd been busy getting to the bottom of Eileen's and Oliver's murders and tracking down the origins of my baby blanket, and I'd taken my eyes off of the baking prize. And now Elspeth thought I wasn't up to scratch. I'd have to dedicate myself to baking all week to get back on track.

I promised Elspeth that I would try my hardest.

"Good," she said kindly. "You're a fine baker. If you truly put your mind to this, you'll excel. Meanwhile, if there is any hint of truth to that strange warning letter, I want you to have this."

She opened up her red Birkin bag and handed me a small tan leather pouch that fit inside my palm.

I looked at her curiously, touching the soft leather with my thumb. Elspeth's bag was very Mary Poppins. What else did she just happen to carry around with her all day?

"It's a fortification charm. The amethyst necklace will

protect you as much as it can, but if danger is imminent, this will help shield you. It's too potent to be worn all the time, so keep it in its pouch somewhere you can reach for it easily. In a pocket or bag will suffice."

"How does it work?" I asked.

"The charm is infused with magic and will protect you."

I thanked Elspeth, slipped the charm into my tote bag, and assured her that I'd keep it safe.

We parted ways at the inn, and I went to my room to pick up my bag and Gateau and carry them both to my car.

It had been another exhausting weekend in Broomewode, but at least I got justice for Eileen Poole and Oliver Jones. I started the engine, and Gateau curled up in a ball on the passenger seat, preparing for a long snooze. But unlike my sweet feline friend, I'd have no time to rest this week. I was going to have to practice baking, and I'd need every second.

Poppy's Recipe for White Chocolate and Crystallized Ginger Scones

Okay, okay, I'm sorry: I know firsthand how frustrating it is to be told about "the perfect scone recipe." Everyone and their dog thinks that their recipe is the best. So I won't frustrate you by claiming this as the definitive recipe. But what I will say is: This spin on the classic recipe is delicious, and you won't regret making it!

Below find my ingredients list and method. If, like Elspeth Peach, you're not a huge fan of ginger, then you can tweak the amounts. Elspeth did say, "I can't fault the scone base itself," so adjust the extras according to taste, or feel free to experiment with new ideas. The basic scone recipe is very versatile, so throw in whatever you have in your pantry and find new combinations of your own.

This recipe will yield sixteen small scones.

Ingredients:

- 1 lb. self-raising flour (2 cups all purpose flour)
- 2 level tsp. baking powder
- 1¾ oz caster sugar (3 tbsp)
- 3½ oz. butter, softened, cut into pieces
- 2 free-range eggs
- a little milk
- 4 tsp. grated fresh ginger
- 1 cup crystallized ginger, chopped
- 8 oz. white chocolate chips or chunks

Method

1. First up, you have to preheat that oven to 220C/200C Fan/Gas 7. (425 degrees) Lightly grease two baking trays.
2. Put the flour, baking powder and sugar in a large bowl. Add the butter and rub in with your fingertips until the mixture resembles fine breadcrumbs. This bit is really important. You don't want it to end up looking like scrambled eggs!
3. Crack the eggs into a measuring jug, then add enough milk to make the total liquid 300 ml/10 fluid ounces. Stir the egg and milk into the flour—you may not need it all—and mix to a soft, sticky dough.
4. Lightly flour your work surface and then turn out your dough. Now it's time to add your extras. Tip

the white chocolate chips and chopped crystallized ginger into the mix.

5. Be careful not to over-handle the dough or it will be tough, and don't be tempted to roll it out too thinly, otherwise the scones will be too shallow.

6. Roll out to a rectangle about 2 cm/¾-inch thick and then cut into as many rounds as possible with a fluted 5 cm/2-inch cutter and place them on the prepared baking trays. Brush the tops of the scones with a little extra milk, or any egg and milk left in the jug.

7. Bake for 12–15 minutes or until the scones are well risen and a pale, golden-brown color.

8. Once cool, slice in half and serve with clotted cream—add some shavings of white chocolate too, if you're feeling a little naughty.

Bon appétit!

A Note from Nancy

Dear Reader,

Thank you for reading The Great Witches Baking Show series. I am so grateful for all the enthusiasm this series has received. I have more stories about Poppy planned for the future.

I hope you'll consider leaving a review and please tell your friends who like cozy mysteries and culinary adventures.

Review on Amazon, Goodreads or BookBub.

Your support is appreciated. Turn the page for a sneak peek of A Bundt Instrument, the next book in the series, and Poppy's recipe for Ginger and White Chocolate Scones.

Join my newsletter at nancywarren.net to hear about my new releases and special offers.

I hope to see you in my private Facebook Group. It's a lot of fun. www.facebook.com/groups/NancyWarrenKnitwits

Until next time,
Happy Reading,

Nancy

A BUNDT INSTRUMENT

Chapter 1

"Ta-da!" my voice rang out as I presented my latest baking marvel to Mildred. "What do you think?" I was pretty pleased with myself.

"Yer cake has a great hole in its center," Mildred said in a horrified tone. "My mistress would have turned me off without so much as a character reference if I'd ever dared serve her such a thing." My kitchen ghost had been the cook here in my cottage during Victorian times and she was always critical of my efforts.

Of course, in her day, losing her job was her greatest fear. Mine was being humiliated in front of the millions of viewers who'd be watching me fail if I got sent home this week. As we entered week four of The Great British Baking Contest I was practicing day and night trying to up my game.

"It's called a Bundt Cake," I told her.

"Hmph. A Blunder Cake more like." She chortled at her own joke. That made one of us.

Gateau, my black cat and familiar, was curled up on a chair beside the stove, watching. Not that she needed the warmth. It was mid-May and I'd be outside enjoying the warm, spring weather if I wasn't panicked.

I was hanging on by a thread and I knew it. I was one 'blunder cake' away from saying good-bye to my new friends on the baking show, and to my best chance of finding out the secrets of my parentage.

I could not let that happen.

I stuck a fork in my cake, which made Mildred even more sour-faced. "I wish you could taste it, too," I told her. I could use a second opinion.

Instead, I pretended I was a judge on the show. I tasted the flavors and texture critically as I chewed. When I'd swallowed, I put on a British accent and imitated celebrity judge Elspeth Peach. "Very good crumb on this cake, Poppy. The raspberry and lemon flavors are coming through nicely. But I feel you could do better."

And she was right.

I looked around my kitchen. It was my favorite room in this old cottage and the reason I'd bought it, even if it did come with Mildred who was full of baking opinions and no help with the mortgage.

This week was something called European Bakes and our first challenge was to make a cake with a European background. I'd settled on the Bundt cake, or Bundkuchen as it was known in its native Germany.

I had bund all over my kuchen and no idea whether the one with hazelnuts and chocolate tasted better than the lavender and lemon, or my current attempt, raspberry and white chocolate. Clearly, I needed someone with a pulse, and taste buds, to help me decide.

I called my best friend Gina to come over. Even if we couldn't choose the perfect bake, we could gossip and she'd remind me that everything was going to be okay.

When I got off the phone, Mildred straightened her mop cap and said, "Well, I know when I'm not wanted," and before I could tell her I appreciated her advice, she'd faded into the old stone wall.

Gateau flicked her tail as if to say, "good riddance."

Order your copy today! *A Bundt Instrument* is Book 4 in the Great Witches Baking Show series.

Popcorn and Poltergeists - Book 9

Garters and Gargoyles - Book 10

Cat's Paws and Curses a Holiday Whodunnit

The Great Witches Baking Show

The Great Witches Baking Show - Book 1

Baker's Coven - Book 2

A Rolling Scone - Book 3

A Bundt Instrument - Book 4

Blood, Sweat and Tiers - Book 5

Toni Diamond Mysteries

Toni is a successful saleswoman for Lady Bianca Cosmetics in this series of humorous cozy mysteries. Along with having an eye for beauty and a head for business, Toni's got a nose for trouble and she's never shy about following her instincts, even when they lead to murder.

Frosted Shadow - Book 1

Ultimate Concealer - Book 2

Midnight Shimmer - Book 3

A Diamond Choker For Christmas - A Toni Diamond Mysteries Novella

The Almost Wives Club

An enchanted wedding dress is a matchmaker in this series of romantic comedies where five runaway brides find out who the best men really are!

The Almost Wives Club: Kate - Book 1

Second Hand Bride - Book 2

Bridesmaid for Hire - Book 3

The Wedding Flight - Book 4

If the Dress Fits - Book 5

Take a Chance series

Meet the Chance family, a cobbled together family of eleven kids who are all grown up and finding their ways in life and love.

Kiss a Girl in the Rain - Book 1

Iris in Bloom - Book 2

Blueprint for a Kiss - Book 3

Every Rose - Book 4

Love to Go - Book 5

The Sheriff's Sweet Surrender - Book 6

The Daisy Game - Book 7

Chance Encounter - Prequel

Take a Chance Box Set - Prequel and Books 1-3

Abigail Dixon 1920s Mysteries

Death of a Flapper - Book 1

For a complete list of books, check out Nancy's website at nancywarren.net

ABOUT THE AUTHOR

Nancy Warren is the USA Today Bestselling author of more than 90 novels. She's originally from Vancouver, Canada, though she tends to wander and has lived in England, Italy and California at various times. While living in Oxford she dreamed up The Vampire Knitting Club. She currently splits her time between Bath, UK, where she often pretends she's Jane Austen. Or at least a character in a Jane Austen novel, and Victoria, British Columbia where she enjoys living by the ocean. Favorite moments include being the answer to a crossword puzzle clue in Canada's National Post newspaper, being featured on the front page of the New York Times when her book Speed Dating launched Harlequin's NASCAR series, and being nominated three times for Romance Writers of America's RITA award. She has an MA in Creative Writing from Bath Spa University. She's an avid hiker, loves chocolate and most of all, loves to hear from readers! The best way to stay in touch is to sign up for Nancy's newsletter at www.nancywarren.net or www.facebook.com/groups/NancyWarrenKnitwits

To learn more about Nancy and her books
www.nancywarren.net